How He Lived an Undead Life

Dr. Scott Young

DEDICATION

I would like to dedicate this work of fiction to all those who love learning about the End Times as I do. There are many who wish to live through this turbulent time in the flesh, yet do not realize this time will be significantly worse than any prophecy teacher may be able to present in any lecture or book.

Introduction

Firstly, I believe one cannot easily jump into this book without knowing much about the End Times referred to in the Bible. Eschatology has been a Biblical hobby of mine for more than thirty-six years, but in the last ten years I have studied it more intensely. So, let's cover the basics.

Daniel 9:27 indicates that there will be a future time frame traditionally called the Tribulation. This will be a seven year long segment of time. II Thessalonians 2:1-9 further explains that the Holy Spirit must be taken out of the way in order to allow the Lawless one to come upon the scene, which is a result of the Church being taken out of the world explained in 1 Thessalonians 4:16-18. Only then can the Anti-Christ be revealed, which is the First Seal in Revelation 6:2. The Tribulation begins with a peace treaty made with Israel lasting seven years.

The event in I Thessalonians 4:16-18, is called the Rapture of the Church. I place the Rapture event before the Tribulation. The Bride of Christ (the Church) will leave this earth during this Rapture event with the Holy Spirit. Some mistakenly believe that the Holy Spirit never returns to the world during the Tribulation, but much of Romans and several other Epistles teach, that the believer in Christ must have the Holy Spirit dwelling in the spirit of the person. Therefore, the planet would have a vacuum for only a few minutes until the next person accepted Christ in the chaos that follows this event, including the 144,000 young Jewish men who evangelize the world in the first half of the Tribulation.

Revelation 9:1-12 has not been taught or described in almost any detail. The above Scripture indicates that people will not be able to die no matter how much they might wish to. We could explain this to mean that someone would try to kill themselves but cannot. I first studied these verses back in 2014, which led me into a survey of the human body, soul, and spirit. This investigation, within the Word of God, gave me a new understanding of the subject of this book which is the understanding of the Fifth Trumpet.

In chapter 9:1-12, we note that the world of survivors will face a horror unknown to man. People will see death turned upon its head. It is my belief that anyone interested in the End Times should examine the tougher portions of the Bible to come to know the knowledge of understanding how difficult it will be for life to exist. Matthew 24:22 states, "Unless those days were limited, no one would survive. But those days will be limited because of the elect." Do not dismiss this verse, because all will be at peril during that future, seven year time frame.

God is trying to get the earth's attention throughout the last segment of time in the history of mankind. If the Tribulation was just about judgment, Jesus could blink His eye to correctly delineate the nature of Godly justice. We all need to understand that the Messiah's death on the Cross *was* the judgment of the universe upon sin. The Lord is seeking all humans to come to a knowledge of Him. At least the acknowledgement of His divine nature to satisfy all of creation. In Romans 14:11 and Philippians 2:11 we are reminded all "tongues will confess that Jesus is Lord."

The End Times real story is the separation of those who will believe because of what He is doing and those who will not believe, no matter what our God does. There will be people who will clearly know that Jesus is the Christ, the Son of the Living God. Even though they will understand this truth they will still completely reject Him and what He represents in this life.

HOW HE LIVED AN UNDEAD LIFE

CHAPTER ONE

"Derek, you're being a putz!" Tarra complained.

"Why, because I am being rational? I thought that's why you first went out with me," Derek smiled a devilish grin that he knew typically melted her heart, but not at the present moment. He changed his tactics in a flash. "I am almost 22, and I will have the money due to me. My dad promised it to me in his Will. She can't control my life forever," he intoned almost like a teenager, to which he still had six months before his money was arbitrarily released to him.

"The Czar has always kept his promises," Tarra hated her word choice as soon as she had spoken it, knowing that the world leader had not said much that had come true. She rationalized that it wasn't the Czar's fault with all the chaos upon the planet. Tarra realized that the world had been indoctrinated to speak these platitudes in the face of the concerns of people's lives. She glanced in Derek's way as she drove the truck along their meandering route towards the cabin in which his mother and the couple had occupied since Derek's stepfather had also died one year before.

Derek was the only one strong enough to hold on to the precious gas cans without them leaking all over the beat-up Ford F160 crew cab. The back seats had been removed in order to hide their cache behind a blanket that was cleverly designed to appear to be a straw strewn and oily mess that would not arouse suspicion by anyone who peered into the truck. The fear of not sufficiently concealing what was inherently valuable always weighed heavily upon their minds.

The Ford was once a beautiful beast, but several intentional poundings by the family, as well as the damage from harrowing escapes on routine shopping trips, this past year, had left the beast less of a target. Paint had spilled in various patterns on the black hood along with the crushing of the hull, which created only superficial damage without real ineffectiveness of the truck's purpose for the family.

An unenviable hole in the plastic navigation system, in the dashboard, made onlookers searching to pick a vehicle clean of its treasures reduce in their minds the value. The hole was actually equipped with cop-busting Bluetooth scanners. Derek's dead stepfather had purchased a glass face to the navigation screen so it gave the impression that it was a non-functional system. Only when it was fired up would anyone perceive the retracting screen that dropped the glass' fake scars. It was one of the many tricks, up the sleeve of the ingenious, but late Kenny Griffin. Derek didn't miss the surly man, but he did forlornly love Kenny's devious nature to conceal technology in plain sight.

Derek's sullen mood darkened further when Tarra had contradicted his thought process. He wanted to be considered as a man who was always right and who preeminently planned his options. In this dangerous time, in human history, Derek felt lost in his manhood when he should have been planning his final college project at the University of Colorado. He had hoped through his project to be selected for a higher position after medical school. CU Boulder was also famous for the best kegger parties in Colorado. Derek, instead, found himself left carrying the gas and the cigarettes as well as the sugar from three separate sources available to those who hadn't chosen the Marker.

"You know that those who get the Marker will be the first in line to have their debt canceled as well as be placed in schools such as the late CU Boulder once classes start up." Tarra was relentless in her hope, because her debt was so astronomical. She knew that he didn't have to worry about school loans with his trust fund coming due, as well as his mother's financial wealth, but she did worry. The mention of CU would undoubtedly have a powerful aphrodisiac effect upon the mind of her budding physician.

"We could sign up on Monday near the court..." The both of them felt as if they were sucker-punched as the gas spilled and Derek roared his worst profanity of the night, which was saying something since he was known for his hilarious outbursts in parties and the way he could cuss someone out in the nicest possible manner. Derek's back slammed against Tarra's right arm producing a curse of her own, as she pulled the steering wheel over careening the truck off the road. But instead of Derek's body completely crushing his lover, his right arm was pinned by the gas cans in the back seat that pulled his scapula out of position, along with most of the tendons in his right forearm. The pain was unbearable for his consciousness to comprehend. Derek was mildly aware of Tarra's piercing screams for someone to stay away from her, because she was "armed and dangerous." The subsequent laughter barely sliced the veil of his thoughts, as he fought to keep his eyes focused in the growing darkness of his mind.

CHAPTER TWO

"Derek, can you get the door for mommy and daddy?" The perfume was wafting through the air that only meant one thing for the young Derek: a babysitter was heading his way. If it were the adorable Gina, he would bask in the glow of her glamour for the night, as he begged her to watch Veggie Tales with him. He peered through the horizontal windows that allowed the visage of the road without the outsiders viewing the occupants due to SR 10 tinted windows. His dreams were about to be a reality, and his body was weirdly responding to the call of the night. His palms were sweating within seconds of jerking the door open in delight over the beautiful Gina gracing him with her presence.

"Hi, little guy," she used a much higher and melodic tenor than she normally did.

"I'm ten now. I grew two inches last year, don't you know?" Derek was crestfallen at the tone of her voice; one that didn't acknowledge him as her masculine equal.

"I'm sorry about that," she patted his head as his parents began the recitation of their nightly whereabouts and their arrival time to be expected later that night. They told Gina that she didn't have to cook dinner because Derek had already eaten chicken pot pie. The night proceeded with Derek playing on his Xbox while she prattled on her iPhone, with her girlfriends, about her hunky date on Friday night. Derek's mood turned more sullen by the moment as the night progressed.

******

"Whaaaat hhhhappppeneed?" Derek reached with his right arm noticing that his right forearm was missing.

The blood was lightly oozing from a jagged wound where his right hand used to be. Finding a towel in the side pocket of the truck, he plugged the gaping stump while pulling back in a cry of pain. He also whiffed the fumes of spilled gasoline soaking all of the fabrics in the truck, including the old blue terry cloth towel that doubled as a bandage for his arm. He then shocked his system enough to understand that the gasoline wouldn't be a half-bad disinfectant for his forearm, even though he took many deep breaths to calm his intense pain. Blood soaked every corner of the truck.

His vision swirled inside the ebbs of agony that pulsed from his newly formed nubbin. As clouded as he was from the open wound, the reality of his loss hadn't penetrated his real situation enough to bring a comprehensible thought to his mind. He peered about the truck searching for evidence of Tarra's whereabouts until consciousness left him again. His blood loss was too dire to keep his mind awake.

******

Derek remembered the last time he had seen his father. It was a Thursday morning when Carl, his father, had awakened him from a groggy state at five in the morning. Carl had to catch a flight and had told him that he loved him. The dead tired ten-year-old mumbled back something incoherent, still deflated from the disappointing night with Gina. Her spurning nonchalance pierced him, launching him into a stupor of pre-teen blues that only brought on more thirst for his gaming into the wee hours of the morning. He had tortured through each session of shoot-em-ups until his parents ordered him to bed for the sixth time as they arrived home the night before.

Carl was a pilot for America Republic Airlines for the past ten years. Much to his father's delight, he had made captain four years earlier. But as a pilot, he had to navigate the waters of non-commitment for basketball games and band rehearsals. Charlene, his wife, dutifully played the role of housewife extraordinaire, a natural role, given the husband she had dreamed of who would indulge her every financial delight, allowing her dalliances with her wardrobe and workout sessions. She had raised a daughter, Angela, who had just entered the University of Northern Colorado in Greeley, working toward a potential career as a lawyer. She was determined to bring her grades high enough to enter CU in Boulder for her Juris Doctorate when she finished her undergrad program.

But Charlene began to resent the absent father and husband bit of a traveling pilot. The captain's chair seemed glamorous to her friends who joked that they could fly the *pleasant jet streams* free of charge, but rarely did Carl wish to venture in that fashion outside of his business. He desired to stay at home. She, therefore, didn't receive the benefits of the captaincy, other than the money. After a few years of the six-figure pay that steadily rose, the remuneration for clothing and material goods was less appealing for Charlene. But that fact didn't stop her from buying on Amazon.com with impunity or any other wild whim on her credit cards. The bill was enormous but manageable for the Fultz family to mount monthly, but there was so precious few savings available for anything other than his pension.

Mother and son were lounging in the living room with hot dogs on their laps, after a long day of shopping at several locales around the Denver area. Derek had also opened up a new controller for his Xbox. Charlene's attention was caught by the muted TV feed of billowing airplane smoke. Peering at the small lettering in the top right hand of the screen that said *"Live."* She frantically reached for the remote to turn it up. She was always worried that her worst fears of her husband's job could be realized.

"Flight 734 was heading for its destination to Seattle, Washington, but was never able to make that landing. We still don't know the technical details of the incident in which at least twenty are confirmed dead, but it seems that the pilot saved most of the crew. Local cell phone videos from this small airport in Montana indicate the pilot was trying to keep the plane level after it swerved to the left," the young dark-haired woman, with a slight British accent, intoned as her hair whipped around her.

"Do we know what caused the deaths?" one of the reporters from the Los Angeles Fox studios asked into the mics.

"The Bozeman airport is too small to handle an A340 aircraft. The front of the plane smacked head on into a concrete guard rail crushing the cockpit before the rest of the plane hit the tarmac. The pilots, flight crew, and most of the first-class passengers never had a chance," the British reporter indicated. Charlene never heard the rest of the report, because her cell phone went off with AR Airlines calling.

She learned that it was, in fact, Carl's plane that had crashed in Montana. They were going to fly the bodies back to Denver once they were extricated from the wreckage. The gentle voice, on the other end of the line, gave her what was supposed to be heard as good news that her husband had saved the flight from oblivion. *All should have died*, but Charlene had long stopped listening as she dropped the iPhone on the sofa in a puddle of tears staining the leathery, beige couch. Derek was begging his mother to tell him what happened until he picked up the phone to hear what would change his life in a moment. The woman prattled on about how *Captain Carl Fultz was a great man and died in the service of America and the airlines.*

The airlines were complimentary of all that Carl Fultz had done to save so many passengers that Saturday, October 6th. The company had already decided to award him their high honor and he was given relative hero status by most of the surviving occupants of the plane. The media continued to sing his praises all over the Denver airwaves, while emails flooded Charlene's mailbox in sorrow and appreciation of her husband's bravery. The two lonely souls also heard that they were giving her fifteen million in compensation, but Charlene's more immediate concern was that the laptop Carl paid the bills from was locked up tight in his basement office.

AR Airlines sent two IT personnel to unlock the unique passwords in an attempt to untangle the mess of Carl's financial status including credit cards, life insurance, and other valuable digital data, so that the family could move on. A close friend of Carl's became the de facto spokesman for the family and took on the responsibility of paying the bills, since Charlene's obvious and debilitating depression was already knocking her socks off. Her hair was profusely tangled because she didn't care to even shower, in the first seven days, except for the funeral.

Carl and Charlene's daughter, a sophomore, fled back to the University of Northern Colorado. Angela had tried to take care of Derek for the seven days before she returned to her campus. By the eighth day, Derek and Charlene sat at the breakfast nook without one of them breaking into tears at the sight of something of Carl's items. His big sister drove back to Greeley after an inordinately long hug. For the next several months, Angela had a seemingly effective support system in her Christian organization that helped her manage her grief.

The family in Denver was a wreck, but Taylor, Carl's friend, played basketball with Derek, as well as took him to practice just two weeks out from the destruction of the family unit. Taylor seemed to have boundless energy for the family's needs having been divorced for one year without any kids of his own. Taylor had come each Sunday to watch the Denver Broncos, only when Carl was in town. The man became ostensibly a part of the family by attending the cookouts on the back porch.

CHAPTER THREE

Derek awoke from the nightmare of his past into the terrifying moment of his present. His pain level had piqued; clearly over his scale of a *ten* which didn't allow his mind any level of concentration. He could not find his right hand and had to take towels soaked in more gasoline to rebandage his stump. At first, he frantically called for Tarra but to no avail. Her purse was also gone. Since he had realized that they were forced off the road, there was nothing to do but go into town for medical attention. He stumbled down the darkened road which had no light at the moment, even from the moon that seemed to be dimmer than usual.

He smelled the overpowering scent of gasoline all over his jeans and on the towel. It stung pointedly on his open wound, but he realized that the disinfectant would hurt like heck but also might reduce an infection. When Derek looked down at himself, he looked paler than he usually seemed late in the summer. He worked outside, so his forearms always had a subtle sheen of brown. That shade seemed to have lightened considerably and he comprehended that he was also presented with dizziness and significant weakness.

Derek loved to diagnose himself in medical terminology which also kept his mind coherent. He couldn't stop worrying about Tarra but knew that he couldn't do anything about her without getting to town. It was a potential two mile walk from Sunshine Canyon to Mapleton Avenue in Boulder. It would take him an hour at the pace he was plodding.

Since the laws had changed in this whacky time of lawlessness, those who didn't have the Marker were punished by death on-sight. The Marker was a requirement to purchase goods it was placed upon the right hand or forehead. The new laws allowed any armed citizen, which seemed to be everyone and his brother, to kill those who were not in compliance with the Marker law.

The most dangerous were those who were authorized as heavy weapon handlers called *Hunters* who were given access to open carry permits. Some of them roamed in gangs with rifles and nine millimeters holstered, passing through any security checkpoint as long as they had their Marker visible on their head and a red tattoo beside their Marker identifying them as Hunters. The extra symbol had become a statement that those who had the Marker on their right hand were fashionable and compliant with the new crypto-currency, but those who plastered the monstrosity on their foreheads were allowed more special access. There were two types of Headers, which was what they were called: Fanatics and Hunters. It was hard to tell the difference between the two groups in their behavioral approach to the Czar of the world, except for the guns upon the hips of the Hunters.

"Gotta stay away from them Hunters," Derek began to preach to himself as if his stepfather, Kenny, was doing so. "Only walk at night...not during the day," he nodded his agreement with himself.

In the distance, he heard screeching tires, as if someone was racing on both sides of the winding street. He was looking for where he could find a Free Clinic that took both unMarkered and Markered. Derek ducked into the trees, wary of being spotted by the wrong people, including maybe the same Hunters who had taken his girlfriend. He felt like a coward by hiding from those potential kidnappers, but realized that he could do little to stop them without a good right hand. The conundrum of cowardice made Derek feel as if the world was laughing at him, while his face bore the signs of a defeated male bravado.

As the vehicle came nearer, Derek noted that no one seemed to be trailing, but it was swaying erratically on its own. With a harrowing speed, it rammed into a telephone pole that must have also had a powerline attached to it. Sparks flew as the red Chevy SUV was totaled in an instant.

The driver must have been traveling more than sixty miles per hour along a turn not commonly traversed at more than forty. The passenger was an unfortunate woman being hurled through the windshield with sickening force. Her head bent sideways and left a dent in the telephone pole. She slowly slipped from the hood to crumple onto the rocky path near the vehicle.

Derek ran headlong into the danger to see if he could render any aid. He had been constantly trying to assure himself that if he desired the bright lights of being a physician, he knew he would have to complete a rotation in the ER. Blood flowed profusely over the passenger's body from her eyes to her neck. Her body also had cuts about her torso, but none of those would be life threatening if it weren't for the unnatural angle of her neck.

The woman on the ground was dead. He then moved to the driver's side, ever so carefully, with his self-protection mode kicking in while trying to help the unmoving driver. The driver was leaning over the steering wheel her right arm flapping in a spastic motion. It seemed to be reminiscent of an upper motor neuron stroke, similar to Parkinson's, but in a much higher movement of the muscle groups. Derek pried the door opened with groans from the side panels giving way by the great effort Derek gave with his good left arm. The woman was barely conscious and slapping at her neck.

"Listen, are you awake?" No response was given, then louder still.

"Hey! STOP IT!" trying to break the driver out of her nightmare of pain. "Do you have a neurological disorder?"

After a minute of waiting for her to come around, she answered, "Yeah, God! Leave me alone will ya? Can't you see that I'm dying?" She moaned. "I gotta have broken ribs. We were just trying to get home when that giant bug bit me. Son of a...! It is *killing* me!" The woman swiped at her neck which had developed red and black pustules that were coursing through her veins vertically up and down.

"How long ago were you bit? And by what, a black widow?" Derek tried to access her history without realizing that he didn't have enough medical understanding to assess the woman. Even though he had studied the medical textbooks for the last two years, at his mother's house, he was unqualified for this. He tried to treat Tarra and his mother, not to mention his stepfather after minor injuries.

"What? Are you blind?"

"Whaddaya mean?"

"They have invaded Boulder, you idiot..." she spat her cuss words and blood spittle in his direction. "I was trying to escape with my wife when I got bit in the car. Is she alright?"

"No, she's dead," then the wails escaped from the woman worthy of psychology textbooks. She would alternatively bawl for her partner and then for her own loneliness, then again for her own pain. He could not make sense of it until she pulled out a gun. "What?! Whatchu doing?!"

The woman turned the gun slowly at the floor of the SUV and then steadily toward her head. Derek was so surprised by the scene that he froze. He had heard that there was a *fight or flight* reaction to pressure, but he didn't realize that one might freeze in the middle of a stressful moment. He had seen his fair share of that. He felt that he should have reacted for her weapon more quickly, but he was still in shock over the nature of the injuries to her partner. Derek did yelp indiscriminately at the driver as she pulled the trigger toward her temple.

He bowed his head in resignation at the brutality of the night in which he now believed would never end. Overcome by exhaustion and worry, he slipped down by the bottom rail of the front door and then onto the pavement. He slumped his chest over and laid his head upon his knees and gave up his consciousness for another time.

*****

High school allowed Derek to come into his own. He had grown four inches in the past year and was nearly six foot two. His blonde tufts of hair were always in position with the hair gel that expertly set it in place, maximizing the effect of flipping his hair up with his pointer finger. The freshman girls tended to go crazy over the affectation of the handsome sophomore.

Derek played basketball as a *two* guard on the varsity team, which allowed him to move the ball in the half-court game so efficiently that he was given the green light to shoot whenever he felt like it. He would drive to the rim and loved to dunk with force or jack a three-pointer. He was scolded by his coach if he tried to shoot like NBA players from deep down court, because ever since the irrepressible Steph Curry launched shots from nearly the half-court line, everyone continued with the ridiculous attempt. Most air-balled the shots including Derek. Courage and bravado on the floor were his strengths and weakness.

Outside the gym, Derek's head was in one of two general areas: girls or the morbidity of life. He focused so much on death that he became an amateur expert, as much as a high school student could possibly be. He would vehemently argue with his friends about their fascination with the Zombie Apocalypse in their spare time around the lunch tables.

"I would get into Walgreens with their access in the corner lot and with their waters and food, not to mention the drugs," Tyler smiled at his brilliance.

"Dude, stupid! They got an open path on the one story. Gotta go up!" Conner smacked Tyler on the back of his head.

"Listen, you boneheads. No one survives in the cities. Now, if you are outside, let's say in the country far away from the hordes of zombies, you might have a chance. But you have to be across a bridge somehow. Once you did that, they would never be able to pass. After a season or two, they would all be dead from exposure or incapacitated. Zombies would die off in two years at most. But you would need sniper rifles and heavy leather armor to decrease the biting, if you did have to get supplies," Derek calmed his crowd with the magic of his wisdom and the dynamic nature of his words, along with the concomitant hand motions indicating that he was in charge of this subject. The arguments raged until Derek's girlfriend, Sandra, rescued him from the deluge of inane comments.

Only at night, staring up from his bed, would he allow himself a moment of solitude from the thoughts of morbidity and girls. Because his mom had brought so many men into their home after his father had passed more than five years earlier, Derek used to laugh at his mother's next conquest. The next several dozen men she brought home made him emotionally shut off his relationship with her. He didn't even bother to know their names, just their faces, so he knew if it was a new one or a consistent romp in the hay.

Charlene had dropped her moral standards so far that she didn't even attend the church that she used to faithfully go too. Her only occupation was to manage her money that counted more than five million, with five more safely tucked in trust funds for Derek when he turned twenty-two.

Derek's older sister, Angela, had already cashed hers in on her twenty-second birthday. She set out with her new family to Portland, Oregon, just after she finished her Juris Doctorate license to practice public law. She wanted to fight against the corporate water rights and filtration systems in one of the most liberal cities in America. Angela felt at home there with her husband, Danny, an attorney as well, and their two kids. Charlene seldom heard from Angela, who hated the way that she was sleeping with any man on the block, but Angela had sown her oats significantly after her father died when she transferred to CU. Their personalities were so much alike that they could not perceive the other's good qualities anymore.

Derek allowed his disgust with his mother's personality to spill over into a strange brew of contempt that was cloaked inside of civility in the home. He knew she had control of the purse strings, but not the path of his life. Charlene didn't attempt to connect with Derek as much as she might have if her husband, Carl, was still alive. She buried her pain inside of loveless relationships and poured her flesh into each contemptuous one. Charlene cried almost every night after her husband's death for nearly a year.

The past didn't slow her down from feeding her new obsession with sex. It drove her. The cigarettes and alcohol numbed the pain from the lack of relationship feelings she didn't have with these random men. She was strangely loyal to one man at a time, bowing to a primal understanding of commitment on some level.

Charlene didn't stay with one man for more than a few months, but the sex was immediate. On some point she knew it was all disgusting to Derek also. She began to realize that Derek had fallen under the same spell by his hormones. He also had a semi-scorn for the lovemaking process. It was clinical and emotionless just like how his mother had inadvertently taught him to operate his bodily functions. That was the pattern until Tarra.

CHAPTER FOUR

Derek awoke beside the SUV to an overpowering scent of rotting flesh and the sound of wheezing from *both* passengers. The blood from the driver had begun to soak his jeans in a ghastly sticky residue that began to chill him. He found a towel in the front door pocket to wipe the blood from his bottom where the woman's fluids had flown underneath him, but it didn't eliminate the stain and smell from his jeans and his nostrils. The odd sensation that took him a little time to odiferously register was the radiator fluid from the engine that leaked profusely onto the pavement. He felt, from the stench of death that he perceived, that he would never be clean again.

He turned back to the woman in the driver's side who was slumped over unceremoniously along the passenger's seat. The oddity was that she was sitting up with only a portion of her gore upon the steering column, breaking all the rules of the cycle of life. She should be gone, but somehow she was not. Her pulse was non-existent which confused the devil out of Derek as he checked her. The driver began to moan loudly with an indicative rhythm of her pain threshold being more violated with each passing minute. In a burst of adrenaline, Derek then decided to check on the other woman, only to find the creepy sensation that the driver's wife was also not dead.

Before the accident, the woman thrown from the SUV would have been beautiful by any standards of the world. Her neck was still in an impossible angle to accomplish breathing. Derek recoiled again in horror as she began to growl in agony. He noted that her airway was completely compromised, and she could not vocalize her needs. He regained enough self-composure to help the woman communicate her needs by re-bending her neck into a palatable order of usage. The screams and appendage flailing flew in all directions as she inadvertently careened one of her hands into his stump, making him cry out in a wail that was oddly in tune with the driver's moans. With her neck in a more reasonable position, the driver's wife went into convulsions, giving Derek the idea that her brain was overwhelmed with the sensations the body was experiencing. He had no earthly answer as to the sickening response to her continued existence in this realm of life.

"Whattttttt the ffffffff?" She couldn't even bring the curse out to satisfy her curiosity.

"I am Derek, and you should be dead!" he intoned the dumbest phrase he had ever uttered.

"Well, I wish I was, but I'm not," more blood arose from her windpipe to clog her words from fully forming.

He looked at her for a few minutes wondering what he might do to ease her pain that was cycling up again as her body began a new rotation of agony. "I am sorry for your anguish, but I don't know what to do. I am not a doctor." If Derek could have brought a laugh up from the depths of his being, it would have been hilarious in the sickest of ways. He was standing with a wholly torn off forearm, around two women who should be dead, from absolutely fatal wounds, but both were alive.

Without an ability to make a difference in the two women's destiny, he smirked to himself at the irony of the situation then scolded himself as he consciously moved away from the gruesome scene. As he ambled down the road to Boulder again, he allowed his mind to wander. It seemed to dull his pain.

The reality playing around him sounded like an episode that belonged on the newly minted horror channel on cable. The channel went far beyond playing the classic horror flicks of today and yesteryear. The new repetition of the horror beamed directly to your chair the latest episodes of *Killing the Saints*. These poor beasties called Christians, by some, were seen in the World Theatre, as the Czar called it, like idiots. They were herded into abandoned ranches with brick walls up to twenty feet high upon a ten acre plot.

A few other natural barricades were erected, along with the dilapidated buildings, which provided a modicum of shelter for the unfortunates.

Trainee Hunters entered with bravado and curses to lure out the Christians until all were slaughtered on 8K TV technology in near real-time. For the audiences of the reality shows, play-by-play announcers from the NFL repurposed their calls by using their skills to explain to the spectators the scenes before them. The announcer replays were gruesome, but somewhat enthralled the rabid fans of the series. Derek had been known to watch an episode or two but didn't care about the reality anymore, because he and his family had become the hunted.

His mother acceded to the wishes of her dead husband Kenny in not allowing anyone who had the Marker on her property. Charlene controlled her environment of the roving gangs that were allowed to kill those who were found without the mark as long as culpable proof was found of the offender's non-compliance. That lurid detail led to the feeling in the Fultz household that they were in prison.

Time passed for Derek as he trudged along the trees, trying to hide his identity from the daylight peeking through as he turned into the straight roads of the city of Boulder. He ducked into side streets' pockets making his way to a clinic that was open to a few of the unMarkered population. Derek reasoned that without his right hand, he might be a bit lucky, because he would not be identified as in non-compliance without the existence of his hand. It was the only time he felt fortunate in this *night that needed to end.* As a new day began he became a little bolder in his wanderings toward the entrance of the clinic and held his right arm to be displayed if anyone looked. Derek's moans grew louder as he approached what used to be Boulder Community Hospital. No one was considering the plight of his non-compliance.

Many with gruesome injuries, much as he had already witnessed, were milling about the waiting room at six AM. Legs that were displaced and seemed to be only oozing a little of their life fluid were flooding into the newly named Uptime Clinic. Derek didn't know why they had such a cheery name for an emergency care room, but he knew if the agency who had called it could see the day in which Derek lived, they would darken the name to something more foreboding.

As he approached the front desk, no insurance was requested from the attendant, which confused Derek, but no one seemed to care. The physicians and nursing staff moved from patient to patient with no emotion or surprise as to the extent of the injury affecting the near deceased individuals gracing Uptime. Derek was pointed to a chair outside of a moaning room that had five much more critically wounded people within them. He was ignored so long that he gave into his tiredness for a needed time of sleep.

****

The first year of college had finally arrived. Derek had a different picture of the day, but the civilization's calamities dampened his spirits. The Czar had swept into power only two and a half years earlier with significant adulation over his ability to finally resolve the Middle East conflict. After Israel was attacked six months before his elevation to the world stage and he miraculously survived, the Israelites were interested in payback on their deposed Muslim foes. Only the Czar was able to broker a peace treaty with the Jews to quash their ability to create a ruckus with their neighbors. The rest of the planet had only known misery in worsening global conditions.

While other parents joyfully moved their children into the dorms, his mother and her new husband, Kenny, hurriedly piled him into his room with little fanfare and left him with a roommate who barely spoke to him in the first few hours of the college experience. Derek didn't care that much for his roommate, because he was more interested in the girls and the parties in the first week of school. CU had typically housed more than thirty-five thousand students, but in Derek's first year they would accommodate only five thousand. Whole dormitories were nearly empty and the campus had a quiet buzz. It was not a pleasant vibe of expectancy that first-year students generally brought with them, but a note of impending doom seeped into the rest of the student population reflecting what was happening within the greater world outside of the campus.

Whole programs had closed their doors to new students such as Audiology, Architecture, Literature, and most philosophy type degrees. The only ones available for new students were the more practical sciences such as Engineering, Information Technology, Pharmacology, Nursing and Medical fields of study. Based on the possible educational endeavors, it seemed the world only needed to keep its technology going and heal the sick.

The kids were all fast-tracked into mostly two-year programs, except for physicians, who had a total of four years before their residency. The other general education requirements of mathematics and literature were tossed aside to push graduates to their needed categories of study, so that they could replace the planet's staggering human losses. More than two billion people had died from so many diseases, disasters, and hatred. No one was immune to the recipe of grief. All pushed down their hardships to create a burden of emotional cocktails leading to barely acceptable interactional standards. There were no more friendly *hellos* along any city streets or in neighborhoods, which allowed each a private moment to process the new set of sufferings that the day might bring.

Derek was enrolled in an amalgam of classes called Medical Chemistry. The budding physician in Derek couldn't get to the meat of the need quickly enough to operate the basics of medicine. He also had Pharmacology for the Physician, Anatomy and Physiology, Human Dissection Part One and lastly, Microbiology for the Physician. It was eighteen hours of massive study that would give him no other time for a job or even a life; he internally mused. He had never heard of so much course work first thing in college. But where there's a will, there's a way for an eighteen-year-old.

The second night on campus, he heartily expected the music to be so loud that he could not sleep. But he noticed only a few had their Bluetooth speakers blaring. He decided to broach the lights from the beautiful campus grounds to find some college action, and he didn't care which kind. Several girls strolled aimlessly through the quad laughing with one another as Derek's curls and good looks came upon the gaggle of girls.

Tarra O'Reilly had grown up in Colorado Springs and had considered going to Yale with her immaculate grades. It was a ritual for kids to ponder the most excellent universities of

America to ply their requested trade with the world at large, but those dreams were summarily rejected by the new government that required state-level freshman to go to the state schools, if at all possible. CU was her only real choice. She was in her second year as a Chemical Engineering major, knowing that she had the breakneck task of a unique three-year degree ahead of her. The course work was challenging, because they loaded all the possible scenarios available that should have been given to graduate course work in that short period. She had none of those easy classes in any semester. College was only for the best of the best minds, while the rest of the population was forced into the workforce of the mundane and dangerous garbage removal and soldiering.

No longer was the USA the national leader of democracy for the world, because that term was thrown into the wastebasket along with Personal IRA's and fat savings accounts that were absconded by the governmental emergency acts. She was a straight *A* student with a thirty-five on her ACT, applicable in other times to any college in America. She would have been on a track to a six-figure income when she graduated with her Ph.D. in Chemical Engineering.

But Tarra's future only held the promise of moderate pay while solving dire troubles for the economies of the world, who had lost most of their fuel resources. Whole populations of people were eradicated, because they consumed too much without giving back into the community what it needed. Africa was a wasteland of wild animals taking back their original playgrounds of existence. The whole continent had reminded the world of a zoo gone mad for the way the animals had killed their human oppressors with vigor.

But Tarra was on the prowl tonight with her girls around her when she spotted her prey in the sepia tones of the failing campus lights. The guy she saw was a beauty to behold with his blonde locks framing a body that was muscular and lean. He knew how to move and what was more important he realized that he had *it*. She needed the type of release that only he could give her before the studies she faced hit her between the eyes. Tarra moved out from her small cadre of girls to head them off at the pass, because this stallion was hers.

"How ya doing, stranger?" Tarra smiled, revealing her innocent but gorgeous dimples that could twinkle in any light.

"Looking for you," he admitted back to her in the same tone. The other girls tried to push in on the new guy on campus, but unfortunately for them, Tarra had locked in for the kill. "Where *you* going?"

"Anywhere we can be together," she flashed another grin of delight.

The two became inseparable through the first weeks of campus life, but their studies required a considerable commitment, to keep in their books, with teachers giving an unbalanced class load to the students.

Professors were tasked with infusing all they could into the kids, who were utterly overwhelmed by the amount of work. The courses quickly required two times more than the busiest college student in the past had to surmount. The teachers were galled by the lack of time they had to bring these kids up to speed. But their new job was to make these kids employable out in the government jobs as well as a few private firms trying to replace their astounding losses of white-collar employees. Professors and students alike knew not to complain, or their collective behinds would be digging ditches in a new third world country like New Mexico.

Some of the professors, though, had a special disdain for the lack of preparedness that these students were getting to enter their fields. The medical fields were severely underprepared for the tragedies that would befall them when the patients with all the maladies of the modern world come and bear upon these young physicians and nurses. They were woefully under qualified to treat patients, but no one had a choice in the educational matter.

HOW HE LIVED AN UNDEAD LIFE

CHAPTER FIVE

A scent of urine invaded Derek's nostrils, and he was disgusted by his waiting room neighbor who peed his pants, but he noted that *his* left leg felt wet. *The control of my bodily functions must be breaking down*, Derek thought. He found a spare paper towel and wiped his jeans to no avail. He decided to lay the cloth over his groin to cover up his most embarrassing deed in public to this point.

"Pissed yourself?" the physician with a British accent rhetorically spit out. Derek was led to a slightly private spot in which the curtains were drawn around him. The doc gave him some mismatched scrubs from the closet above Derek's head. "Change into these."

Derek did as he was told as quickly as he could, as the physician wasn't leaving the room. After examining his right stump, he injected a numbing agent into one of the veins closest to the wound that might be intact. Within almost two minutes of debriding his forearm, Derek relaxed on the bed.

"Feeling better, are we? Well, you'd be one of the lucky few. I am Dr. Felix, and I gotta see what we can keep of the rest of your arm here.

Sit still now." Derek reminded himself that he loved the Australian accent as the pain began to set in. It was becoming harder to concentrate the more that man worked on his stub, which also brought on a great sadness such that Derek could not control bursting into tears. "Hey now, bub. You should be thanking your lucky Czar you can't feel anything. All of our drugs are not working for the past twenty-four hours."

"Why is that?" he suddenly sobered to ask the question.

"Only one idea, but it's kinda crazy. We have noted that when we put drugs into anyone who doesn't have one of those reddening sting markings, they cannot get the relief from the drugs. If you have been stung, there'll be nothing to fix them up. You don't have one do you?" Dr. Felix continued to dab.

"Stung? Who is stinging whom? No, I guess not."

"Are you outta it or something? Listen, I am sorry, but I really have ta remove this," Dr. Felix raised his eyebrows to refer to most of his forearm where the physician was making a slashing motion upon Derek's arm.

"NO!"

"Yes. There, there, pumpkin; it'll be right as rain. Tell me how you hurt yourself?" as Derek searched the ceiling for the answer that wasn't coming to him, he noted a prick of pain under his right arm, and then an IV that was placed in his left wrist. "I'll be back when the block has taken effect." Dr. Felix was gone in a practiced second after Derek looked around the room to scan his environment. He then noted that his head was too heavy for his neck and he bounced onto the pillow to sleep again.

****

Just when Derek was enjoying the work of school, the Dean of the School of Medicine called the medical students to a meeting. The first, second, and third years were wondering why the fourth years, as they took an informal roll call, were not among them. The murmur about the room hinted at the foreboding as they entered the hall near finals in May.

Fifteen minutes late for the scheduled time, the students swung their heads toward the right to view Dr. Pillars pushing through the double doors with a non-confident stride. It was something to behold, because no one had ever spied the erasable Dr. Pillars off her game. She ducked her head not making eye contact with any student who searched in vain for a hope that this meeting might give the desperate students good news. Expectations were dashed by her first utterance.

"I am sorry, my awesome students," she paused to drink from a cup that was beside the podium and coughed. No one had been referred to as *awesome* before, because that would connotate that they were outstanding students. Derek knew some of them were holding on for dear life with the challenging course load. Derek was one of the few students who was excelling in medical school. "I regret to inform you that the university is closing at the end of the year. Those of you with student loans will be required to start repayment in September, by law with the new standards of governmental plans of payback." Dr. Pillars began to stumble over her words, as the whispers grew in intensity she drank a little more from her cup.

"Listen!" she bellowed in her familiar tone to attain control of the room as the verbal noise rose in volume. "It sucks. I am out of a job, though I may get to live on campus for a time longer. I had tenure, and my retirement plan is now up in smoke. I am on the streets just as much as you are. The fourth years will be graduating in a private and cheap ceremony on the quads. Please be respectful of their work. I know you have all worked very hard though!" trying to hush a rabble that objected to her choice of the word *work*.

"But the Colorado state budget has dried up. There is no money coming in from the state. We are not even going to get paid our last checks. You are going to have to find a job under our global savior, the Czar, of whom I *adore*. He is wise in all his ways," she rose her right hand in the traditional salute to the picture behind her of Czar Nicholas, who graced the hallways of every government building in the world in gaudy art. One of the photos in the medical wing showed the Czar nude as if he were recreating the statue of David by Michelangelo.

With her jutted hand outstretched and her head bowed in prayer mumbling nonsensical ramblings, the rabble was reduced to the same mutterings Dr. Pillars completed. Since Derek was not allowed to be Markered by order of his mother who held the purse strings for his education, he adopted the other pose of putting his palm outward over his forehead to indicate his respect.

If one received their Markered symbol on the hand, the salute adopted by the century-old Nazis was instituted as the sign of adoration to their savior. Conversely, if one chose the unique honor of having a Markered symbol on their forehead, the palm out and bowed response was appropriate. Derek was tattooed with a symbol that allowed him to move about the campus without being accosted by the fanatics who hunted anyone without the Markered points of inclusion. He was safe, because he required no funds to pay for his college thanks to his father's money that came from an increasingly crazy mom, Derek noted to himself. Dr. Pillars left without answering one question but had handouts for those who needed to know how to repay their loans as their duty to the Common.

"Do we even go to finals next week?" Colleen asked.

"Why? School's over. It's not comin' back!" Trevor threw his pack up in the air without caring where it landed or if it was retrieved. The sentiment was precisely the fear that all of the students, who were out in the cold, could have repeated if Trevor hadn't beaten them to the punch. They separated experiencing the first stage of their grief. Derek skipped over the denial stage to move onto the cocktail of depression, with a side order of anger, by kicking the chair beside him. All of their dreams were completely dashed.

Only thirty minutes later, Derek found Tarra wandering the quads with tears falling profusely. He understood that she had been informed of the same decision that he had by her dean. They walked in silence as the emotions raged within the couple. They ambled together within their swirling depression that threatened to swallow them. Each time one looked at the other for confirmation or hope, that their situation may not be as terrible as they imagined, the other's blank stare crumbled their vision of a possible future in their chosen fields.

"If I could have just finished my engineering! I would have a job. As it is, I am done for until they reopen the campus. When do you think...?" she asked Derek who only pulled her close under his armpit in acceptance of their shared fate.

They had been living in the 1000 square foot cabin that Charlene had built for the two kids coddling their vision of a future in each other's embrace before their destinies unfolded. She didn't want him living on campus in the second semester, because the meal plan was shut off and so was the water in the dorms. All of the students had perceived the impending closure of the school. Twitter was abuzz with the news of the reduction of higher education worldwide. But the whole nation admitted that people were dying on the streets from unknown, antibiotic resistant diseases. That fact relegated the strain of campus closings to inconsequential. Some countries, such as Japan, had lost their entire governmental infrastructure without access to the outside shipping lanes that had forgotten them after they lost power from a nuclear meltdown in three facilities. The population was losing its hair, en masse, due to a global ailment and not enough medications to staunch the flow.

HOW HE LIVED AN UNDEAD LIFE

CHAPTER SIX

Derek awoke to the acrid taste of bile that had backed up in his mouth and vomiting on the right shoulder of his scrubs until he turned his head enough to put the rest of his stomach's contents on the floor. There were so many people in beds so close to his that it was as if they were having a giant sleepover, as he would do before his father died. He, therefore, didn't know if the upchuck was the stinky man beside him, who had run out of deodorant two months ago, or his own stench. The caking mass on the floor was so embarrassing that he wanted to clean it up. Derek's problem was that he finally noticed that his right arm was in a sling with an IV attached to his left wrist.

He could not feel much from his hand but hoped that they had found his right appendage to reattach it. Derek wondered if someone had put it on ice as they did in the movies. He might still be able to live with the dream that he could one day be a great physician healing the prettiest of girls to their undying adoration. That was when he realized the stupidity of his prodding by placing his left fingers upon the wound without cloth resistance passing through the area where his right hand would have been.

The flood of consciousness came to him through as a blood-curdling scream escaped his lips. He was a one-handed man who would need help to button a shirt.

"How's that upper arm feeling? We gave you versed. Most of these hags would have killed to get a little of that juice in their veins," Dr. Felix patted Derek's leg as he spoke.

"It's gone!" Derek retorted the stupidest message he uttered.

"Yup, buddy. That's what happens when we perform an amputation. Sucks but you are alive...sort of," the physician broke off his reply oddly.

"Whaddaya mean *sorta*?"

"You had almost five pints of blood missing from your body when we did your surgical assessment. You shouldn't have been able to walk in here, but everyone's doing it," the physician explained.

Derek was too confused to reason his night out, then he noticed the light peeking through the blinds. "What day is it?"

"Thursday. The 18th."

"It's been four days since my car accident? You gotta be kidding me!" Derek began to feel a wooziness rising until he lay back down again.

"You've been out for two days. We are pumping fluids back into you. Again, you are one of the lucky ones. For those who were stung, we cannot find a line to pump anything in if they have bled out like you. If they have their fluids, nothing will decrease the pain. So, you weren't stung which again is more fortunate than the rest of these people," Dr. Felix gestured to the rest of the bay of patients moaning and groaning about Derek.

"That's right. Is that why those women along the side of the road were still alive?" Derek quickly explained the accident with the two women who should be dead but were still moving around.

"If those women were stung, I think so. Each person who has been bitten by these yet unseen beasties are unable to die or receive pain medication. The agony can ramp up to unbearable levels creating severe toxicity. But again, that's a guess, because you are still alive from your accident. You should be dead..." Dr. Felix trailed off.

"Whaddaya mean you *guess?* Aren't *you* a doc? I was in the middle of my schooling over two years ago at CU. I have learned a lot from books but really wanted...*want* to be one."

"OK, Derek. Here is what we know. We know if you are stung that no medication can make a difference for the pain. The chat rooms are using the term *Zombies*. The Zombies are coming here for insane treatments that should work but somehow do not. Then those who are not Zombies are talking to Zombies to find a way to do it," Dr. Felix ran his hand through the side of his hair in exhaustion but didn't seem to be in any hurry to leave Derek's side. Derek wondered if his bed was the doctor's break.

"Wait, you keep using the word *Zombies*. Are they watching zombie movies or playing games? I don't get it."

"Zombies are the new term for those who should be dead, but they aren't. We think when the stinging hoard showed up, they changed the body chemistry of the world."

"So, how is that possible?"

"We don't know. They call you guys, who died without being stung, the *UnDead*. The Zombies are those who were stung but are trying to kill themselves or are attempting to find a way to create fatal wounds, but they still don't die. The world's gone completely insane," Dr. Felix then began to spit obscenities as if he were having an epileptic fit. The two men sat beside each other attempting to process their portion of the information and coming up with a course of action that each needed.

"Do I have blood back within me?"

"No, sir. We cannot give you blood. Each time we try to infuse either the UnDead or the Zombies, we see a coughing or vomiting reaction almost immediately. Sometimes it even comes with an IV, which is why you spit up a little bit.

Not as bad as some, but we keep learning more each hour. We are, therefore rewriting regimens as we speak by experimentation. The UnDead, like yourself, and even the Zombies, begin to convulse as if I am putting battery acid in their veins. I didn't even try it on you. Now, we can put fluids, we think, and you can drink or eat, but we don't know why blood is so toxic to the UnDead or the Zombies. That's really all I know. If you want to help out a little with your training, we could use your help even if it's one-handed," Dr. Felix offered the first bone in medicine that Derek had ever had and one that he had desperately wished for. If it were proffered up only days ago, he would have jumped at the chance — if they didn't check for his Markered placement.

"Uh, well, thanks, but I gotta find my mom and girlfriend. I don't know where my girlfriend is after the crash. I'm gonna make my way back to them. But after I figure it out, I'll come to help you out," Derek offered.

"Sounds good," Dr. Felix patted Derek's left hand and removed the IV to discharge his patient. He bandaged up the hole in his left hand and moved on to another patient. It didn't seem that anyone cared for money at the moment. *Maybe, this clinic was privately funded,* Derek thought. He didn't care what the mistake in getting his personal information was, because he was going to duck out of the line of fire of those who might seek that type of documentation from him.

But as Derek moved to find some more scrubs from the drawer, that he had pilfered in the past from, he noted that no one was focused on anyone else. Each person was focused on their own suffering. In the past few years, Derek reflected that the sideways glances were against those who were not conforming. If one was in the wrong, be it not praying to the Czar or operating a business with the Marker protocols, then Hunters might show up at one's door to eliminate the offender.

Initially, one of the worst visceral responses toward law-abiding citizens was being pulled over by the police for speeding or receiving the dreaded tax audit. Similarly, his mother had been audited sometime after his dad had died, and the experience was nightmarish. The full review cycled through three agents and two managers, not to mention encompassing several years in which she had not filed the proper taxes. Somehow, his father hadn't provided the correct forms which caused the harassment of their lives, but audits were more invasive in the present. Only four years earlier, the threat of tax repayment or potential imprisonment would have been a joy compared to the dismal response now when government agencies were targeting their citizenry.

Seizure of land, homeschool of a child, or due process with the ever-changing laws of the land were met with destructive force by the Hunters. Doors were broken down and people were hauled away to detention camps. Businesses could be ransacked and closed without even the media presenting the resident's side of the case. No one cared about the legal processes in which one had a fair hearing; justice was a lost art in the land of America, not to mention the world. Of course, the breeches of impartiality had been replaced by the extreme civility toward the criminal, at least in the minds of Derek's parents around the dinner table when he was young. The rapid changes were dizzying and deadly at the same time.

With his arm in a sling, Derek seized the time to reflect upon the behaviors of those within the clinic. In most hospitals, patients could be doubled in number by those who were being assisted by family members. It seemed that the balance of patient to assistant had shifted to a ten to one ratio.

It was disturbing how much pain a body could handle. Derek had studied the dopamine responses within the anatomy that provided for a respite of relief, but those inhibitors were shut off for inexplicable reasons. Gunshot wounds turned tan mini-couches in the waiting area an angry red. Massive head traumas were laying upon the floor holding their brains with their hands. *This can't be happening,* Derek thought to himself as he chose to leave the clinic to reduce the horrific sights.

Instead of going back the way he came upon the road to his mother's house, he chose to move deeper into Boulder, meandering on Mapleton, and then turning south until he reached Pearl Street, where the city life had popped in the middle of the town. All the unique restaurants and shops were located in the heart of Boulder. Since the tragedies of the past several years had hit the businesses so hard, no place was unaffected. So many of the eateries were boarded up, but they were still susceptible to break-ins taking anything of value. The few firms that were open seemed to have turned into a real-life Zombie Crawl.

In Denver, when Derek was in high school, he had persuaded his friends to dress up as some of the scariest of zombies on Halloween night. If one were outfitted as a convincing undead, store owners would offer higher discounts and the Light Rail in Denver would provide free services to those participating. All of the kids were dressed in the genuinely disgusting, which pleased Derek to no end. The behaviors were a study in horror as each person incorporated the costume as a persona to exhaust those who wished to be terrified. Derek loved the waves of morbidity on that night each year, because the physical images of death echoed the darkness, left within his own heart, after his father was cruelly taken from his presence.

Thursday night on the 18th of September, the leaves should have begun to show their colors, as well as the CU Buffs taking the field against UCLA. All Derek beheld is the revisiting of the Zombie Crawl in all its authentic brutality from which Derek couldn't take his eyes away.

One young woman had lost the left heel of her four-inch stiletto footwear that potentially indicated her age-old profession. The loss of the heel had left her with a severe limp. She wobbled through the crowd screaming for someone to end her pain. Derek could not view her malady until she craned her neck to the passersby who paid her no attention. The left side of her neckline had puffed up to two times the size of the right in which she held her hand to supposedly reduce the growing pain. Her wrists were freshly splayed open and oozing freely down her yellow, low cut dress. As she moved her right hand away to hold back who might have been a potential customer as of a few weeks ago, Derek spied what appeared to be her carotid artery purple from having been emptied. She had lost all of her fluids.

Another older man, in what seemed to be a tailored to fit business suit, tugged on his tie for the tenth time trying to create a distraction for his agony. He picked up a discarded shotgun that Derek hadn't noticed and expertly loaded a round in the chamber. People around stepped back three paces as he opened fire upon his chest.

The blast propelled him back into an abandoned newspaper receptacle that hadn't been used in what seemed ages. Derek was the only one who moved forward to help the poor soul with the shotgun blast. But as he sidled up to Mr. Business Suit, the man wiggled on for ten more minutes. Derek gasped at the man's intestines which were spilling into the Pearl District like they belonged to the street. Blood and guts were strewn about the plaza for all to experience in its ignominious nature. Within twenty more minutes of Derek wandering about the district, five more rounds rang out in the night in various directions. No one was gaining relief or respite from their wounds, just a more profound amount of suffering after trying to finish the kill job of oneself.

Derek decided to remove himself from the carnage, playing out like a video game that he had frequented throughout his youth, to a small coffee shop of anguished people. Only one person was selling the coffee, without regard to her safety and seemingly outside of any pain that the rest of them were experiencing. She poured cup after cup for the poor souls that didn't seem to culminate in relief. A chatroom was displayed on a rather large laptop that was garnering much attention and catcalls.

"Ask them how to kill yourself. I can't stand it!" A teenager younger than Derek pleaded without the benefit of an ear and obvious auditory trauma based upon his volume which was significantly louder than the background deserved.

"I am, you moron! But I don't want to zombify myself!" the woman without a noteworthy wound howled back at the hearing-impaired youth.

"What do you mean by *zombify?*" Derek cut in.

"Were you dead this morning?" the controlling woman of the keyboard asked.

"I was out of it in the clinic getting my right hand cut off three days ago," he retorted back.

"Well, sorry, but you don't know then? We are trying to find a way to die. If you were stung in the wave that hit Boulder a few days ago that lasted almost seventy-two hours, then you would have known that all of us were stung. We cannot find relief. We cannot dose up with any medication or the favorite illicit we used before."

"Can you get rip-roaring drunk?" Derek offered.

"Done that. Didn't work," another turned to him and answered, from recent experience based on the overpowering smell that reeked from his pores and mouth. He was probably a long-time alcoholic, Derek surmised.

"What stung you?" Derek asked. "I didn't see anything and didn't get stung."

"These little horses that screamed out bit me. They had long hair and looked oddly human, albeit kinda small for a human that was melded into a horse figure not even four feet high. I bent down to pet it at first, thinking that it was some genetic experiment gone wild. It bit me on the shoulder through my coat," the laptop woman pulled her shirt back to her bra line to reveal an oval-shaped bite mark that seemed to penetrate her bone leaving her with more than four inches torn off of the surface of her shoulder.

"Did they leave?" Derek asked those gathered.

"I guess. Some didn't get bitten, and we are not exactly sure why. But we gotta have relief. It's been two days for me, and I gotta find a drug. The next step is zombifying I imagine," an older man in his fifties showed his bite mark upon his own Markered section of his right wrist.

"Wait, you said that it was screaming. What was it saying?" Derek recollected with a snap of his left hand which reminded him that he would never do that again with his right.

"They all were screaming, 'Zombie Trumpet! Zombie Trumpet!'" two of the men intoned together as if in harmony of a memorized song of yesteryear.

"What does that mean? We are invaded by Zombies?" Derek asked utterly confused.

"Not the Zombies I saw in the movies. Now, we are the living Zombies but have some of our faculties. If we don't feel a release, no one is gonna make it. It's driving me crazy. I can't sleep, eat, or drink. I drop everything that touches my lips unless I sip it from the table," on cue the man mimicked his process of sipping coffee without the use of his violently shaking hands.

Each of the people, in their increasingly troubled state of mind, retold mostly the same story. They saw the creatures muttering to themselves until a person came near to make sense of what was said in their native tongue, because all were hearing it in their language. Once they moved close enough to the odd creature, a lightning speed reflex exuded from their mouths to sting each of the affected in that coffee shop. They kept repeating that Derek should count himself lucky that he only lost an arm. Derek's faculties were being flooded with opposing messages, not allowing logical explanations for the insane world about him. As the group muttered their questions to their computer host, to search *Google,* for references to suicide that were successful, Derek backed his way out of the coffee shop unnoticed.

CHAPTER SEVEN

Before medical school, when Derek experienced bloody incidences, he mused that he would have to get used to the insides of man. He realized, as he walked out again into the once beautiful Pearl District in Boulder, that he wanted nothing to do with this level of blood and guts. Bile rose in his throat at the nauseating aroma of roasted flesh from gunshots, spilling urine, from the inhabitants of the District who could not restrict themselves, and the vomit in the corners of the buildings. It was more than his stomach could contain. He allowed the sputum to mix in with the pooling blood by the destroyed newspaper stand that was overturned by the shotgun blast. The newly Zombified man still wriggled beside it.

After he finished with whatever might have been ingested, he moved on from his nightmare of Pearl Street to find sanity. Returning north to Mapleton Avenue, and then toward his house to the west of Boulder, he retraced his path to find Tarra. He spotted a woman in her early twenties tipping from the top of a four-story building. Before he could respond to her plight, she toppled from the structure; her diamond earrings glinted in the moonlight as she fell.

The fall lasted only a moment but felt like it stretched into minutes from the horror of the consequence. During that tumble from the building top, Derek inwardly asked any deity who might be listening for help, even though he had lost hope of believing in anyone who cared about the world anymore.

He jogged carefully to her side with the aching right arm telling him that his pain medication was starting to wear off. He knelt at the puddle of the woman assessing her wounds beginning with her feet. Her left ankle was bent backwards due to the nature of the fall, as her feet impacted with the ground first. Somehow, her hip was also rotated in the opposite direction from how Mother Nature intended, Derek clinically quipped to himself. But he quickly moved up to the face that was surprisingly intact, because the rest of the body had taken the brunt of the tumble. He backed away for a moment realizing that he knew her. She was in one of his medical classes back in college. He searched her face, desperately trying to place her within his past.

"Oh, Shelley, I hope that you found your release," he sighed out as he pulled the lock of hair from the middle of her forehead. Knowing that she would need to be buried and hoping that she was dead, he moved her hip awkwardly until she stirred with the howl of a wounded animal. He had never heard another person make the instinctual noise that Shelley produced. She began to thrash about, making her hip flop like a Band-Aid that hung on by one side. Her lower leg also bounced off of the pavement spurting blood which must have been released from her femoral artery. Without knowing how to treat her, he applied pressure to staunch the flow of blood. But the mere touch from him made her cry out harder in an utter agony. He had never seen or heard anyone experience such a horror. Derek searched about him with desperation for help until he realized that he was one block from the clinic.

Before he could reach the front doors that were still packed with the living dead, a man with a shotgun and an ugly wound that took off most of his ear and portion of his jaw, stumbled alongside where Shelley lay. In a moment of complete clarity, he straightened up to aim his weapon into the head of Shelley. Before Derek could stop the man or even scream out, the man turned awkwardly, without some of his face, toward Derek. He spoke something that Derek could not hear due to the gun blast.

"What?" Derek asked. More mouthing of words. "WHAT???"

"I SAID I REDUCED HER HEAD TO A PUDDLE. SHE WON'T HAVE TO THINK ANYMORE!" Then the man's pain returned to his face as he moved toward the Pearl Street death that Derek had just evacuated.

Derek gashed his knees grinding the knee caps into the pavement which was the least of his physical worries mixing his pain, emotional and physical. Shelley's brain began to spread out upon the ground, soaking his jeans further with more gore. He sat in utter shock over the day without a concern for his anguish which was steadily ramping up.

After several minutes of crying for the loss of her neural function, he noted that Shelley continued to spasm uncontrollably. Then the jerks of the exhaustion came with a more frightening consequence; she pounded the asphalt in what Derek believed was a form of communication. No sounds emitted from her being, because all the blood was expelled from her body. She could not speak with her speech anatomy missing.

"I'll post that as another Zombie," a shaking young woman snapped Shelley's picture with her Samsung phone. "She's not going anywhere. She will have to lie there until..." The sentence was never finished as the woman moved on in her distress with a welt that ballooned out of the side of her exposed jeans. She had cut away her pants to allow her wound to breathe, but it only pulsated. She touched it and winced with each step. The casual nature of death initiated a new level of Traumatic Stress that could not be calculated by the survivors of the past years of disturbances where loved ones were lost all too frequently. The odd scene of the woman sickly fascinated Derek when she posted the photo to the web for reference to indicate how *not* to kill oneself.

"Dead but not dead!" the woman quipped over her shoulder only fifteen feet away. Derek then passed out in shock of the immense trauma and his amputation that could not be ignored.

****

Six months after losing out on his CU experience, significantly short of his degree, Derek was still in a funk. His daily tasks, at his step-father's hidden cabin outside of the city limits of Boulder, began early in the morning. He fed the chickens just before dawn; then he shoveled the manure of the horses, chickens, rabbits, and pigs from the fields. The dung was loaded upon a flat space outside of the dusty barn that was purposefully not kept up. Kenny Griffin asked that Derek's mother, Charlene, take on his name to protect her from the prying eyes of the "commie government pukes" that Kenny would nightly decry.

Kenny was a millionaire by his own making, as he retired from flying with the airlines, which was one of the attractions for Charlene replacing her dead husband with Kenny. He had invested in so many of the risky options, in the early years, of some of the most expensive stocks in the NASDAQ, which made people wonder if he had insider trading information. The past experiences with government agencies purged his patriotism for the country he used to love in his piloting days, for the Navy, and then as captain for several commercial airlines.

"Don't have their navigation within the cars, ya hear me, boy?" Kenny would regularly require his help with handing him the correct tool for the car repair. None of his vehicles were less than thirty years old, except his favorite truck in which he had spent thousands altering the navigation system into useful tools for his needs. "They'll track you down in an instant. That's why we hijacked our phones, so that the navigation is not active." Kenny used old IsoToner gloves on each engine block, so that grease from one portion of his repair would not taint another part of the motor. He wanted a long life for the vehicle. He seemed almost obsessive in his cleanliness with the cars. Each truck had its pair for the job so that they would not *cross-contaminate.* Derek didn't spare the time to pay attention to the ramblings of a conspiracy theorist on every subject.

Derek's days were dreary with work. The internet was heavily protected by severe encryptions that Kenny had spent a fortune on restricting, so that the family could peruse the news of the day. The problem for a young man at age twenty was that there were no jobs, and the few that were available were akin to waste extraction. With the strict controls of his mother, who held his dead father's purse strings, as well as his new step-father's requirements of living off of the grid, he had precious few options available for the mind that he was developing.

He chose to use his time wisely, while not working for the household. He would devour any textbook or article that he generously purchased from medical information sources. The family knew that having Derek understand the nuances of medicine could save a life in the perilous times on the acreage. His respite from living on this makeshift ranch was his weekly jaunts into Boulder for the particular needs of his family. They soon became 007 type missions to avoid the police which delighted Derek in the cat and mouse game he took great care to play.

Most of the time the police were not looking for the intermediates of those off the grid. The furtive eyes of the guilty and the happy-go-lucky careless people who were clueless as to the changing rules of the land were the easy targets of the authorities. The ones who were so afraid to pass a peace officer walking on the street were identified readily.

All knew by this time in American history that lawbreakers were subjected to the harshest consequences. In the past, the liberal media would decry the death penalty for all criminals including the most heinous of felonies. But in the last two years, Derek had seen the uptick of relatively petty offenses and their concomitant punishment meted out by the Hunters in their execution.

In the Old West of the late 19th century, lawless towns had to dispense with their own brands of justice, in brutal formats, so that the safety of the people could come with a modicum of peace. When the violence had ratcheted up, significantly from time to time, duly appointed sheriffs would deputize many of the townsfolk to enforce the laws with deadly consequences. Derek noted that the Hunters were the modern version of the deputizing by the government. They had to be licensed to *open carry* a firearm, through a rigorous process of loyalty that had nothing to do with the soundness of one's mind. Once they were deputized, they were given considerable bounties to roam in various communities to ply their trade. They were armed with specialized automatic rifles that only the military had access to, along with nine millimeters on their hips.

Before the crazy time of the world, in which millions of people went missing in a blink of an eye, the Hunters would have been gang members, pimps, and ex-military men who had lost their sanity inside of their own drug-riddled past and pain from their illegal trades.

In the new loyalty based time frame, each Hunter wore black and was as mysterious in their dealings with the town as their colors would indicate. It seemed to Derek that an excessive number trolled Boulder until he traveled to Denver to procure more precious supplies with his family. The groups of roving Hunters seemingly increased exponentially in the larger cities. It was then that the family knew that their days of going into town indiscriminately were quickly drawing to a close. But that was when the unexpected came to pass.

The street of Colfax in Denver, in the 1970s, had a seedy reputation for violence, drugs, and prostitution. The people would avoid Colfax unless they needed to frequent the area on Saturday mornings to find bargain parts for their wares including hard to find items. In the 1990s to the early 2000s, Denver had chosen to renovate the sordid past of the thoroughfare. Within five years, almost no one could recognize the development that had been the worst portion of the city, along with the explosive growth that would continue for the next twenty years, throughout the metroplex area. Those challenged to procure items were still found, though on Colfax. Therefore, when several repair parts for the ranch were needed, the family ventured into the heart of the authorities of Denver who could arrest or summarily execute his complete kin by the gun barrels of the Hunters.

A dilapidated structure that probably should have been torn down in the seventies seemed to exist beyond expectation just a quarter-mile off of Colfax with multicolored paints upon the exterior walls. The last coat of primer was a forest green, and a stairway ran down, almost unseen, to people who were not aware of the nature of the shop below.

The family delicately traversed the flight of steps to cover the sound of their tracks, careful that no one would be conscious that they were trying to purchase goods without the Marker. These underground facilities tended to be located behind an inadequate entrance with customers who shopped so quietly that whispers were the preferred volume of communication. Above *Jerry's* was a deserted Mexican food chain that died, along with most of the private businesses of the world, when almost a billion people disappeared from the earth years before. Within a minute of entering the store, a man greeted them with a phrase that meant nothing to Derek.

"What would the Czar think about that jumper?" the hidden eyes of the clerk asked.

"He would hate them, but he hates me too," Kenny retorted a line as if he had memorized it.

"How can I help you then? I am Doug Warner," he paused for the name.

"Kenny...thank you, Doug. I need a few of the basics," Kenny and Doug were off with a quiet jovial nature of two peas in a pod. Derek wasn't terribly interested in the conversation, because he wanted to scout about the fascinating place. Upon the shelves of *Jerrys,* books and supplies were organized in a pattern of orientation by their relative application to the customer's possible catastrophe: Disaster Preparedness for Today, Earthquakes, Tornadoes, Water Supplies, Medical Supplies and a host of other topics with packed shelves of materials that were all dusty. There were no clean surfaces of yesteryear's storefronts. In Derek's present, unsoiled wares were still valuable. Derek spent the next hour searching the medical texts and supplies to find a few that would fill in his gaps, be they need to his toolkit or medical information. He didn't even notice the brunette beside him until he smelled a familiar perfume.

"Tarra?!" Derek's voice cracked in utter shock. "It's been almost a year since school. I could *not* find you!" He began to sweat with anticipation of lustful images of college bringing a sober response to the world's current condition more than passions. She flung herself in his arms.

"Oh God, Derek. I've missed you. I went to live with my dad down here in Denver until he got caught last week. They executed him on the spot, but I ducked behind a dumpster until it was over and cried until the sobbing abated," an evident sadness washed over her face as more tears leaked out behind those beautiful blue eyes that had so enchanted him. He also missed her ability to speak with such descriptive words when others were so common, which then reminded him of the ever-present dullard Kenny.

"I got home quick enough to get a few things and some cash but had to leave, because I heard the sirens dashing closer to our hideout...my hideout. I guess...someone else's hideout now," she mentally swerved off into the memory of her father.

"Come with *us*! Kenny and mom will take you in. Your chemical engineering background could be invaluable," he lied because he didn't care why she would live with them, other than that she would be in his bed. They hurried to find his mother and explain the situation in hushed tones. Charlene was sympathetic to her plight but was not able to quell the feeling of her son's passion for the girl before her eyes. She nodded her assentation to the plan to bring Tarra into their home. Kenny was another matter entirely though. Derek and Tarra anxiously awaited the decision that seemed to come with a few heated words. But when they both noted the tale-tell signs of surrender, with his arms in the air, Charlene put the thumbs-up sign to the kids from across the store.

Within minutes of his life-altering experience of bringing his love back into the fold, he was on cloud nine for the rest of the day. Charlene and Tarra conferred on her ability to help out in a variety of ways, including Tarra's supposed fantastic ability to cook. No one claimed to cook well without having a little ability actually to do so. The proof would come in the pudding, as his father used to say when he was alive. Tarra coyly placed a large roll of cash into Kenny's hand and thanked him profusely as she joined the family without ceremony.

CHAPTER EIGHT

Derek's stump had ramped up the agony to a level that awoke him from his fitful unrest. He noted that his arm had been slightly exposed and rubbing against the pavement where he lay. His face was wet from the anguish that he felt in his right arm. He picked himself up with a grunt and realized that he wasn't more than a mile away from the Boulder Community Hospital, where the rest of his arm was removed a few nights before.

"I gotta get there...I gotta get..." Derek trailed off, willing himself to brave the steps that only groans could express. He was on a short-term mission to procure the pain pills that he forgot to fill as he left the hospital in a stupor.

He internally jibed at his gait, repeating the famous words of his favorite commentator, Chris Berman, who had long ago retired from ESPN: *rumblin', stumblin', and bumblin'.* Only Chris Berman could make the NFL plays that were pedantic to the viewer and create magic. It was one of the few memories he had of his father who would watch the ESPN football highlights on a nightly basis when he was home.

Derek used to sneak his way to the couch, even in his onesie pajamas with Star Wars characters upon the body of the clothing, and plop down beside his father. His father, for his part, would wrap a right arm around his son as the two watched in silence, or alternating laughter, the Sunday game highlights shown with Tommy Jackson and Chris Berman. The energy he felt, from the recollection, gave Derek the strength to make his way to the clinic where he found the pharmacy desk.

The clerk barely looked up as she pulled the script from the bluish fake marble countertop. He would wait in torture as his pain cycled from a ten to a fifteen on his own described scaling. There was no one in the waiting room who didn't find themselves past a ten. The few that entered through the doors with lesser injuries, after surveying the wrecks of humanity, quietly removed their wounded selves to bandage their own injuries at home.

The loudest screams or the biggest gushers would be seen in order. The staff seemed to be in shorter supply than even two days earlier. After hugging the wall, upon the floor for more than two hours, Derek passed two hundred dollars into the woman's hand, which was a huge overpay for their forty dollar meds, that in the days past would have only cost fifteen. He didn't need the questions, but his slight smile, referring to his amputated right forearm, reduced the suspicion of the pharmacy clerk as she pocketed the cash without a second glance upward. Without a water fountain nearby, Derek choked down two pills with a little difficulty, as he sat back down on the floor. He closed his eyes for ten minutes waiting for the cyclical pain to abate. When it had reduced, he could then focus his eyes outside of his own misery.

"Man, you must be blessed by the Czar Cartiff above!" a man with only two bloody fingers and a shattered forearm motioned at Derek.

"Doesn't he also go by Supreme Chancellor Cartiff?" Derek tested Bloody Fingers.

"Yeah, he does. But, I use the more effective title of Czar. It's more comforting and reminds me to praise him daily. Don't know why, but what I do know is that those who follow his deeds closely enough, in honor of his godhood, love to utilize that moniker," Bloody Fingers trailed off as his pain began to cycle up more fully.

"Uh, yeah, I didn't know that. When I worship, I only heard the Supreme Chancellor name. I don't get a lotta news," Derek's lie was relatively blatant, but Bloody Finger's agony was dimming his wits. "Wait, why do you say I am blessed?"

"Cuz you have some relief with pain meds. That means you were wounded before the Zombie Apocalypse hit us. I was bitten on my left arm here and tried to shoot it off. I couldn't stand the agony. All it did was worsen my grief. I feel every nerve coursing up my arm now. Don't know why adrenaline doesn't kick in. I had those pain blockers before when I tore my ACL three times playing college football for the Buffs," Bloody Finger motioned eastward toward Folsom Stadium, as if they could see it outside the window. But anyone who had spent any time in Boulder knew that he was talking about the Colorado Buffaloes. Derek looked him up and down, noting that there was a powerful build to Bloody Fingers, along with a growing flat tire around his waistline.

"Zombie Apocalypse?"

"You outta it, son?" Bloody Fingers pushed up his right eyebrow in the inquisitive nature that only Dr. McCoy, on the old Star Trek movies, could do when he was puzzled. His father could replicate that genetic look that Derek couldn't emulate.

"Yeah, out for days while they took my stump down after a...an accident," Derek nearly allowed his truth to seep out about his truck flipping several days ago. He seldom let anything slip, as to the details of his life, in the way that they were. If one person could put together the minutiae of his existence in Boulder, they might find his family. Who knew if the man was a cop?

"That's what the Inter-Tube is calling it. People are trying to die, but they can't. If you have been bitten by those sons..." he trailed off in clenched teeth pulling in on himself until the pain cycled back to a potential level of repose. "It's not gonna let ya die."

"What's not gonna let you?" Derek couldn't shake his confusion with the lack of particulars the man was offering. As he was about to answer, a nurse grunted his name, which made Bloody Fingers forget about his conversation as he ran into the admittance area to be seen. Derek realized that his opportunity had passed to learn more of the truth of these new circumstances of life. All the rest of the people wailed the moans of non-communication. The question and answer session was over, and Derek realized that it was his opportunity to veer out of town with a portion of his dignity still intact from his suffering in the Boulder Community Hospital.

CHAPTER NINE

Derek stepped out of the clinic into a cold chill that wasn't there a few hours earlier. All who lived this close to the mountains realized that a temperature inversion could ensue within a few hours, reversing a day of good weather. The storm and cold fronts rolled over the Rocky's and could back up snow against the foothills to pile up quickly. October was in full bloom, and the trees had already lost their colors for the year. The nature lover had also suffered from the continual forest fires that burned whole plantations of plant life about the beauty of Colorado's High Country. Within the last several years, since the Supreme Chancellor had taken power over the planet, there had been too many natural disasters to count. All had taken their toll on animal, human, and plant life alike. It was enough to drive a balanced person to psychosis.

Those thoughts raced through his brain as he noted the reduction of hidden agony ramping down to a *five* on the pain scale. He hadn't felt this good since the accident at least a week ago. Then his thoughts went dower as he considered the loss of Tarra. Derek's eyes began to flow in a steady stream blinding his path. She could be dead in a ditch, wandered into a hospital, or even taken by a sexual pillager. The last one filled him with an incredible amount of dread that he could not shake, until his senses returned to the sequence of the previous week.

"Why didn't I consider that?" Derek almost slapped his right hand to his leg, in a learned motion from his dead father, whom he mimicked at every chance. A new track was formed in his mind that external predatory behavior would most likely be curtailed by the nature of the global experience of personal excruciation.

Men who took to cure the sexual power demons within would be suffering mightily concentrating on their mortality. A smile formed on the side of his lips as he considered those who had sought to torture those about them for their own private gain. "Or as my dad would say, 'Ill-gotten booty calls would die,'" Derek quipped aloud, though he had to admit that he had embellished his father's comment of *ill-gotten booty* adding death. Dad's old sayings still rang out in his memories.

The walk toward his broken truck was arduous in his weakened state which hadn't included food in the more than three days that he had been awake. He was ravenous, but the throes of those around him had diverged his path from his own physical needs. Ten to twenty steps could be surmounted before he sat beside a road sign, tree, or guard rail of Mapleton Avenue, as the thickening trees and dead brush, turned into Sunshine Canyon Drive just outside of Boulder proper.

The excursion also made quenching his thirst just as vital to his energy reserves which were depleting too quickly for a young man of twenty-one years old. He was in too good of shape to be this tired. The sureness that the torturers of the world would be more incapacitated drove his hope to new levels of confidence he only had in his mind, if not his body. After three sets of breaks, he could not trek on without a snooze.

****

Angela was his big sister, whom he admired, and her leaving was what had eroded his fragile confidence as a sixteen-year-old. Angela had met a man who filled her with the hope that she could start her career in a low paying job in her preferred destination of Seattle. It was a hotbed of activity for a left-wing political idealist with a law degree looking for a voice in the world.

"I have to get out of here with my man," Angela looked up at her baby brother who was taller by six inches. She tasseled his hair, as she had done when he was younger, while he pulled away. In those early years, she had been the anchor during her summer breaks, but those memories were too long ago for Derek. He didn't want to be treated like a kid anymore.

Tears forming on the edge of his vision, Derek retorted, "You're gonna leave me with her?" Derek pointed toward the half-closed door of Angela's room that would become an exercise room or a guest bedroom, so that their mother could entertain more men than he could count. Her romping days with a new man knew no bounds, until she could not remember the man's name the next morning. She was able to be loved for a moment in time that was always more fleeting than the last. That fact was even evident to the high school Derek.

Angela would move away to Seattle and settle in a two-story home that cost upwards of a million upon the hills of the upper-middle class just south in Renton. She wanted to strip the country of all the democratic ideals to plant her desired flag of socialism in America. Her radical speeches in the back halls of justice rang out, a young voice of one who could rally the younger generation to action, against the nature of the republic on which the nation was founded.

There were deprivations of millions who were picking up the pieces after the rabble-rousers thumping their Bibles had left the planet. No one was unaffected by the mass vanishings, but freedom died in the voices of those in whom Angela stoked the fire of socialism. She hoped to allow for the betterment of a society that had no resources to combat all the poverty that came with the collapse of the free markets after the disappearances.

Angela was winning the battle, while her long-time lover was physically pulling away. She came home one night after seven PM to two scantily clad women who were strutting for her man's pleasure. Their submission made her sick to her stomach as she exploded for the raunchy party to end. The response was more confusing than she imagined as they laughed at the death of Angela's relationship.

"Ah, come on and join us. No? Well, now you know the truth..." James bellowed.

"And it will set you free!" one of the submissives preached to the laughter of the threesome.

"Get out!" Angela screamed with a louder but less sure voice than before, hoping for acceptance of her place within their bungalow abode. The girls looked to their superior who shrugged his shoulders.

Angela, at first, believed that finding him unfaithful would end the debauchery, only to find out that he reached out for his desires to be rekindled anew in front of her eyes. James would again return to the chained embrace of his girls as the giggles from the girls renewed. When she caught them back in their bedroom, the cadre ignored her sobs from Angela's throat and continued their wanton lusts.

Angela drove through the streets of Seattle, finally parking her car near CenturyLink Field that housed the old Seattle Seahawks when the NFL dominated the mindset of those downtowns. The field was in massive disrepair, as the homeless took up residence in a shelter off of the fifty-yard line.

In the past, she was with her cohorts in political activism working seventy to eighty hours a week for the bureaus of change. She could find herself all over the city with relative safety, which she could never comprehend, but paid little attention as to why. Only later would she find out that their tattooed foreheads had bought them protection aligning themselves with the world's new governor, Chancellor Cartiff. Angela procured for herself a pink tattoo along with her Marker.

Her words were ushering in his presence, block by block, in a populated city that had seen so few of the disappearances, unlike other American cities. The coasts of America became countries all to their own with separate mindsets of consciousness. The disappearances also lost the trucking from sea to shining sea.

In her stupor of rejection, Angela didn't care about a predator or a mugger as she wandered the area. She was already violated in her home, which was a veritable home invasion of her private sanctum. She could not imagine a more profound attack until the reality came. Angela was jumped by four men who were on her in a moment. They tore all that she had left to her, until her bloody being was bare for all to witness. No one came to her rescue. Her picture was uploaded to the database of those who had died on the streets of Seattle, as if she was just one of the killed in action, in a violent war-torn society. The irony was not lost on Angela, in her dying breaths. She had brought on the terms of her finality, upon the earth by creating anger and resentment wherever and whenever she ranted in public.

HOW HE LIVED AN UNDEAD LIFE

CHAPTER TEN

Derek pulled himself up, as the pungent odor emanating from the roadside invaded his consciousness once again. He first whiffed his right stump only to realize that it had its putrid smell, but he then noted that the road was giving him the new sensation. Only two yards from where Derek lay for his sleepy time, a body was in grotesque repose in a style he had only witnessed in horror movies. The man was in his forties in a vertical red striped pullover sweater and torn jeans. His Markered right arm was above his head, as if he was reaching upward in a yoga class to stretch his limb. He was graciously shot between the eyes and appeared unresponsive.

Derek couldn't help himself as he checked for vital signs. The man was white as a sheet and not leaking any more blood from his horrendous wound that had bled down the embankment creating its creek. From closer inspection, the ghost seemed to resurrect with a wheeze and a word that was unintelligible. Derek asked him to repeat it and only on the third refrain was it understood.

"Zzzombified, shoulda paid more."

"What should you have paid? What's your name?" Derek asked, trying to assess the man's capability to respond. He repeated it two times louder until heard.

"Calhoun, stop whispering will ya? All I hear is a roaring! Can't you make it stop? Kill me!"

"Calhoun, who did this to you?" Derek screamed with a boom that could surely be heard down the road.

"Hunters. They're friends...had 'em take me out. Only had to give them the next score up to the road in return," Calhoun railed through clenched teeth and seemed to be missing a few. Blood began to spurt between his lips again, but in a brackish color that he had never seen before from a live human. In the past week, Derek imagined that few were actually alive on this earth.

"Hunters? Who'd you give them?" a panic hit the heart of Derek thinking that his truck might have been the mark. When Calhoun didn't reply, and one of his eyes rolled back into his skull, he knew the answer wouldn't be forthcoming. The beginning of this mess was around the time of his car accident on Sunshine Canyon Drive, only a few minutes in a vehicle ride into the wooded area outside of Boulder. Once his calm had returned, he decided to leave the poor fool. No charity or compassion was feasible for the fellow.

After hours traversing the winding path with only one car that passed, Derek didn't even stop by his truck, making sure that no one would recognize that it was his. He ambled forward until he reached the underbrush path in which one had to move a steel fencing that laid on its side, barring the driveway to his mom's house. Since he was on foot, he could maneuver around the barricade and trek up the hill far from view of anyone from the road, because it looked like an abandoned trail to all passersby.

In a day and age when the forces against his existence threatened him each time he traveled to town for supplies, he loved how effective his dead stepfather had regraded the driveway into the circuitous path to seemingly nowhere. But on this day he needed the straightest of trails for his weary body, he cursed each step with new invectives that made him chuckle ever so slightly. The discomfort had ratcheted up another level or two, as he had swallowed his next dosage of pain meds. Derek reached for the door but fell through the opening into the waiting arms of his girlfriend, Tarra. Relief flooded his being as his body finally gave out its strength from the arduous journey only five miles away from town.

Tarra had called for Charlene to fetch Derek from the porch, but Charlene could do little to help Tarra lifted him to the nearest couch. Charlene was favoring her shoulder and arm from the welts upon them from her own sting.

All were weary from the chores of just surviving another day in the upside-down reality of an extended apocalypse that no one had ever predicted. Tarra didn't ask him any questions but plopped down beside her man on the comfy couch that could accommodate two adults if they lay upon their sides. Both dropped into a fitful sleep as Charlene crunched into her favorite chair with moans that would have stirred the dead, if there were any available in the city limits of Boulder. Consciousness dripped away into fitful dreams of the damned upon the planet.

****

The ranch was the most satisfying time for Derek, outside of CU, where he was robbed of his chosen field of medicine. He had reconnected with the beautiful Tarra. He could not resist her naturally curly brown hair that was set to the side almost regularly. Her hair style enchanted Derek with lust for her as well as a desire to protect her. Her eyes were a hazel that sometimes turned green. At times, he would remark to her that they were different shades, depending upon the light. His first communication in college with her related to that observation.

"Hey, your eyes are green!" Derek leaned over in the campus bar that was louder than most dance clubs. The beat pulsed into the chest and could restart a heart if it failed.

"God, that's the worst pick up line ever," Tarra intoned as he gazed into her eyes during their first date. He was a cross between Leonardo DiCaprio and Matthew McConaughey. She reversed the line meant to push him away. "But I love corny lines by one such as yourself," she reinvigorated the smile that had faded from his lips. She had been hooked since she had spied him on the quad in his first week of school.

On the ranch, Derek and Tarra found that their love was passionate to the point of being too loud for the house requiring space in the bunkhouse. That fact was perfect for the lovebirds who decided that they would marry each other in the wilderness of the estate that they cohabitated with Charlene and Kenny, both of whom seemed to be ever-present. They initiated a private ceremony with no one attending, but both were wearing their Sunday Bests. They exchanged their form of vows which didn't include their perception of the arcane Judeo-Christian vernacular about abstaining from others. Tarra and Derek knew that their lives were intertwined with lust and fear which could lift from their existence once the terror threat of the world backed down to an Orange level. They fooled themselves with their brand of immaturity in their life circumstances.

Even after the young couple continued their relationship on a new level, the sexual tension in the house between the mother's love and son's love was almost comical, if it wasn't so unhealthy for the four of them. Tarra and Kenny, for their part of the triad, tried to find ways of removing themselves from the rivalry inside the blood relatives' displays of affection. The competition of passion was a motivation for Charlene and Derek. They were continually trying to outdo the other on more levels than were comprehended, even when card games were initiated by the foursome.

Tarra would quickly shut off the exhibition under the pretense of fetching tea for Kenny who would beeline to the kitchen to prepare the sugar for his beverage. All parties learned that separation was more necessary for the mother and the son in anything other than the essential conversation of the ranch work to separate the growing hatred for the two blood relatives. Kenny perceived that the relationship was dissolving into a boss-employee interaction that was uncomfortable in what wasn't being said inside of the clique of the four. Kenny resorted to secret communications with Tarra with upraised eyebrows that indicated that they both wished that the insults would fly as missiles toward the mother and son, instead of the con the two engaged in each day.

But work would invariably interrupt the tension, because the ranch demanded their attention day and night with its own set of invectives. Wolves and other predators were starving in the woods about the ranch. The berries and prey were conspicuously absent over the past several years. Four years earlier, as the Supreme Chancellor Cartiff took office, after the historic peace treaty in Israel that shocked the world, the world was reeling from the disappearances which were a great mystery. The thought police arose out of the chaos to redouble efforts to squelch the rumor mills that had video evidence of people warping into thin air. The new theories gave rise to the conscious thought of beaming technology that was Star Trekian in concept. Scientology stepped in to proffer that theory which took hold since it didn't interfere with Cartiff's plans.

The World Counsel presented a group of grey and white aliens who were warring against one another for dominion of the planet. The grey aliens were seen as desiring a greater good for the earth to lead humans into an age of rebirth. The blame for the millions of beamed away fell upon the white aliens who were trying to warp people into a new existence of an alternate universe. Numerous documentaries were hastily produced to indicate the puzzle of the planet between the two opposites of Greys and Whites. Each time the Whites showed up in folklore, they were pretending to be angel messengers from a God who didn't care about humanity, but had a nefarious memorandum to stop with the work of peace. The Whites' goals were to divide the people into denominational groups based upon the silliness of a mythological book called the Bible.

More mainline docudramas played the same underlying theme of the deception of the Whites bringing mankind into a dogma of hate speech against those who stood for acceptance of their fellow man for all his quirks. The inclusive nature of the World Neighborhood, that Supreme Governor Cartiff was conveying, was impressive to all but Kenny. He didn't like any government, in any shape or form, and his word carried upon his land. He was a powerful speaker who could create the most persuasive coffee house arguments to sway Derek and Charlene in his direction, for a while at least. Tarra wasn't as sure about Kenny's views about the government in the strength of his hate for them. But, she wasn't willing to trust them after they killed her father, so the family, thrown together by blood and marriage, stuck together. That was until Kenny died.

CHAPTER ELEVEN

Kenny had asked Derek to help him haul a load of milk and eggs into town to barter for gasoline and ammo. The ranch produced more milk than the four could utilize, as well as eggs from the chickens. Kenny squealed *chickees!* Each time he called them, in a falsetto voice, he surely caught each animal's attention. The eggs were set upon the bed of the truck that had an old mattress below it to soften the bumps. It was gently tapped down with cartons above, so that the eggs would not bounce around and break.

"But ya gotta know as we set 'em that we'll only lose about 10% of the haul to transport issues. Price of doing business this way," Kenny's brand of wisdom was chagrin and earthy. Derek didn't contradict the man since he didn't know any better regarding the nature of moving that many eggs to town along with the milk in the back of the truck. They turned into the Boulder city limits but were forced to slow down. At first, it seemed like the police were cordoning off the area to which they needed to flow. Kenny started to cuss softly under his breath with Derek, confused by the scene. "I'm not gonna get caught in this heist."

"Whaddaya talkin' about, Kenny? I know we don't want to get caught by the police, but we haven't broken any laws yet. They just came out with the voluntary Marker qualification for business transactions. You don't need it to trade," Derek offered.

"That was eighteen months ago...too many changes in the legal interpretations for my bones. But that ain't what I'm worried about. This ain't the police, young in'," Derek hated it when Kenny treated him as anything less than an equal. Of course, Derek had to do the work of a man, but he was never given the respect of one. Noting the questioning glance of the boy, Kenny proffered. "Don't you see that they don't have their shirts tucked in all the way?"

"I guess, so?" Derek intoned irritatedly.

"Bud, you're gonna die if I'm not around ain't ya? I'm a guessin' I need to take the bullet for you," and in one felled motion, Kenny unbuckled and put the truck in park. "You are the man of the family now, keep your pretty mama safe. Move over into the driver's seat."

For Derek, the whole event was clipping at three times the speed of sound. He couldn't tell why his step-dad was so jumpy and moved out of the vehicle. The truck was old enough that he needed to slide just a few feet over without lifting his leg too much to move into the driver's seat; putting his hands on the wheel in utter confusion. Kenny was talking to two of the men in blue when a plethora of colors emerged from the bushes and trees to the side of the road. Voices were raised as Kenny motioned a wave at Derek to get behind him as he put his hands upon his head. Without considering, Derek slowly moved out of the old green truck, without closing the driver's door and backed out with a pistol in hand.

Somehow, no one was paying attention to Derek's passage away from the chaos. Derek tiptoed in his best *Mission Impossible* interpretation to exit the scene which was turning more dangerous by the moment. He slipped into the underbrush with little notice, because Kenny was speaking so loudly as to appropriate all the attention of the men and women seeking Kenny's end. With laughs, they brushed his bangs from his forehead with a nine mm and moved his glove from his right hand to note that there was no Marker upon it or his forehead. Their intent was clear; they were Hunters meaning to collect on a bounty.

In the past year or two though, Derek's family had noticed that they were not always Hunting murderers, but those who hadn't submitted to the authorities for their Marker were now included. Hunters might pass by a rape or looting event to capture the more in-depth subject of their prey finding a small, non-threatening family trying to slip by in town. The ransom was much higher, up at five thousand dollars per forehead and right hand that they turned in without the Marker, which denoted the lack of compliance. Derek watched the crosshairs of a nine mm point at Kenny's head as the leader pulled the trigger nearer his mouth. They didn't want to mar the forehead to lose their reward. The celebration raged on after the shot was heard including weapons firing off toward the trees. They took Kenny's truck, with its treasures of eggs and milk, with the cadre of their Hunters including Kenny's right hand and forehead as their proof.

The tears that fell from Derek's eyes were only slightly directed at the horrific scene of the mutilated body of his mother's husband who was always a pain in the rear. The rest of the flow was in pure terror for the brutality that he could also possibly endure at the hands of the Hunters. The sacrifice Kenny displayed was now the fate of all those who even turned themselves in. It took almost ninety minutes to trek the six miles back to his ranch without the patriarch of the family. He continually ducked behind trees, waiting for passersby to cruise into town.

The meeting in the house that night was met with wails from both the women, who held each other, leaving Derek feeling so helpless to protect the two women he held dear. They wanted to cry and share what they remembered about Kenny's quirky behaviors that had served the family so well through the almost two years they had all occupied the ranch. But the property was his mother's, and he was trying to con his mind into believing that he could protect the ladies.

******

Normally, Tarra adored rising next to Derek, but on the couch all she smelled was necrotic flesh. There was a whiff of disinfectant spray mixed with dead and burnt skin emanating from Derek's right stump that he lay above his shoulder on the sofa protecting it from being touched. The odor was so unpleasant that she extricated herself from his semi-embrace to the kitchen. Charlene was also fitful on her recliner, because she oozed from her numerous wounds keeping her in constant agony. Mother and son had little conscious thought for the next two days. Collectively, they would take no water unless it was dribbled onto their lips from tablespoon-sized portions given by Tarra. She had also been stung but was feeling a little relief in her new-found research.

As Tarra considered what she was discovering about the malady that had hit the world, only the internet had quality information, which reduced the symptoms of agony to a dull ache. Fascinatingly, she barely ate, because the moderate activity of eating produced more pain than the pleasure she used to experience. Tarra was only 5'6" but weighed just a shade over one hundred and fifteen pounds during college.

After she was stung, like most of the population, her weight had reduced to under a hundred. She was looking more like skin and bones.

Without the pouches she hated around her belly, which she chided herself for losing, she loved the lack of fat she saw in the mirror. But the rapidity of her weight loss was still concerning. She could not eat with much regularity without diarrhea and vomiting unless it were the blandest diet she could create: rice, eggs and apples. Too much salt or sugar created severe cramping that held her on the toilet for thirty minutes until she could finally lift herself into a more dignified position. Her repose on the toilet, though, was the least of the population's worries when the agony of the bites was on the loose.

Charlene groaned inside of her slumber as Derek pulled himself from the couch to splash some water upon his face. Soap took too much effort but was needed. Therefore, Tarra slowly began to wash his face and hair in the kitchen sink, while Derek laid his head on the granite counter to cool his feverish forehead. He noted that his pulse was racing like a boxer about to be battered in the ring by a completely outmatched opponent right before the fight. He must also be battling a post-op infection, along with the stump that was oozing a fluid that he was too afraid to check fearing the worst. He then realized that he reeked to high heaven, which instantly made him self-conscious around Tarra.

"I am so sorry about smelling so bad. I know you hate to be around me when I am this putrid. Wait, you are never around me when I am this gross."

"Ah, it's ok," she whistled and realized that she didn't mind the odor in her attempt to help her man, unless she was right under his armpit.

"But you can't stand it when I smell," he jerked his head up flipping water about the kitchen counter.

"I know. I couldn't. Maybe I still can't, but somehow it doesn't bother me. Ask me why," she excitedly pulled away while he took over the reins of wringing his hair out with his left hand.

"OK, shoot," he didn't have the energy that she seemed to muster.

Tarra began to pace about the kitchen while he leaned against the countertop. "You remember that night, don't you?" to which he nodded, knowing the exact reference. "The SUV was unrepairable after the accident. I woke up minutes later and searched for you in the wreckage. Once I found you, I wept for what seemed hours. You were dead. All of your blood had drained from your body while your right arm hung at your side halfway attached. I checked your pulse. I was frantically trying to breathe life into you. You were gone!"

"I was?"

"Yeah. I didn't know what to do. I had spied that a huge red truck had forced us off the road, but they were gone when I came to. Some of the cash was gone as well. They left us for dead, which seemed to be the case in our condition. I had a concussion that knocked me out," she pointed to her head that had a larger Band-Aid upon it which galled him that he hadn't asked her about her own injury. With a motion of his left hand, he gently brushed her cheek to apologize without a word. She leaned her head toward his hand to acknowledge his gesture.

"Anyway, once I came to the disturbing fact that you were gone, I sat upon the pavement with gas soaking my jeans, in my despair, unable to move when another vehicle slowed down. This kindly older couple, about in their late fifties, ran to my side to assess my wounds and dabbed my head with a towel they found aside the road from our destroyed SUV. The woman helped me to my feet and gently guided me to their sedan into the back seat with her. The husband tended you for several minutes, valiantly trying to resuscitate you, to no avail. He then dropped his head for a few more moments, while he touched his hand to your bloody chest. When I asked her what he was doing, she brushed my forehead to move my bangs, but I now know that she was checking for the Marker. I was apoplectic and uncommunicative while this beautiful soul soothed me as I lay in her arms," Tarra paused her story to reminisce. Derek's pain was ebbing away inside of her charming use of highbrow wording to explain herself. She could really tell a tale to captivate him.

"Well, I only awoke again at their house as the woman, Heather with fiery red hair, again guided me up the steps to their front porch. Her husband, Dr. Tony, dutifully jumped in front to open the door for her as they pulled me into their house. I felt no compunction not to be led away to a strange house with the peace that was filtering into my being," her countenance beamed as she spoke.

"How long ago was all of this?" Derek interrupted her story.

"About ten days ago. You have been gone for that long. I was with them for five days, as they nursed me back from the concussion. Anyway, I sacked out in their guest room for about a day or so until I felt like I could move. They kept waking me to check on my condition. Dr. Tony was a physician before the Tribulation as he explained it."

"Tribblation?"

"No, you, putz, not tribbles like in Star Trek. *Tribulation!*" she smiled at the way he seemed to be joking, only to realize that he hadn't heard her correctly, so she explained her new level of wisdom.

CHAPTER TWELVE

"Tribulation means that the world will end, I think, but I don't know the specifics. Anyway, back to the story, after I awoke, I was out of my mind for the first day with my pain level scaling so high. I couldn't stop crying," she referred to his stump which recreated the consciousness of the pain within his arm all over again. He stepped back into the living room to pull the pills from his jacket. Tarra helped him open the bottle and got him a glass of water, so that he could swallow it as well as a little goat's milk. Tarra almost instinctively reached out to rub his right arm that was closest to her, until she was reminded of the aching stump that poked out from his rolled-up shirt on the right side.

"How do you know all of this? Have you been reading on the site with those crazy prophets in Israel? I checked them out, and while they seemed credible, they were too circumspect in their logic," it always amazed him that he elevated his vocabulary when he would attempt to match her wisdom which spewed forth with ease. She had been a voracious reader all of her life and doubly so without the TV on in the household. The foursome had come to feel that they could not stand the lies that the media was spilling each day.

"Heather and Dr. Tony gave me the answers to life. After I argued with them for a couple of days, their logic was impeccable. I...uh..." she paused and rounded the kitchen island to psychologically put distance between her most cherished human relationship in the world fearing the retort that might come from his lips which could crush her.

"What?" his head was starting to become a little fuzzy, while the pain ebbed down to an *eight*.

"I have become a Called...a Saint for Christ."

"What in the..." he paused a moment but exclaimed the cussword anyway, for extra emphasis, and then repeated. "...you talkin' about?" He instantly noted that his life flashed before him, as if she were now the enemy.

"I worried that you might react that way," countering as she spoke, pushing farther away from him as he began to bridge the distance. He was a big man, and she always cowered when men became angry. It was a byproduct of her father in the tactic he would take when her mother or Tarra's sisters would disagree with a position of passion he felt. Tarra's father's logic could make one run for the hills to duck and cover. The feeling, when it cropped up with any man in her life, made her countenance shrink to a dwarf. "But I am not backing down on this one," she blurted back to him.

Completely confused when she tended to take this type of reactional state, "What are you talking about now?"

"Did you hear the words that I said? I believe in the Jesus of the Bible. They showed me the truth of His Word, as they called it. They walked me through the death and resurrection, in which Jesus had to die for our sins. They indicated the path by which, in John something or other, Jesus had died a death that could not be faked as the Muslims believe He was. Did you know Jesus had plasma leaking out of Him?" the last question brought her on the offensive with her rounding the island.

"Plasma? No, wait...why is that important?" Derek asked suddenly curious about a medical reference.

"Because it's been there in the Bible since it was written, but we only discovered it in the 1930s. It's a perfect proof that the Bible has been true all this time. I refused to see it at first, but they laid out the truth in consummate detail. Hey, wanna meet them? They invited me back!" she excitedly retorted.

"What about my mom?" He changed the subject.

"She won't eat or drink anything since she was stung. I have tried for days to dribble a little in her," they both exited the kitchen to check her out on her favorite recliner in which she was immobile.

"Oh my, Go...." Derek trailed off. He gently bent down to find a way to attend to her multiple wounds.

"I know..."

"When did all this happen?" Assessing her injuries, as a doctor might, he began to tally the sites of disfigurement.

"While you were asleep."

As Derek lifted the gauze wrap that had at first looked like a scarf around her neck, he noted she had a slice that ran from ear to ear and was three inches wide along her neckline. Tarra explained that all of the carnage occurred over the days he was passed out on the couch. "She jumped off the railings and has broken her collarbone. She took the shotgun to her stomach before I could hide it, so that she wouldn't do it again. She also slit her neck. I bandaged it, so the blood isn't oozing anymore."

Charlene's wrists were even slit on both sides, vertically and horizontally. Huge bruises puckered around her collarbone on the right side, injuries sustained when she supposedly launched herself from the open balcony they had upstairs, her bedroom perch from which Kenny liked to see anyone coming down the road. He couldn't imagine how she was alive until he reminded himself of the woman along the streets of Boulder who had dived from a church steeple splattering on the pavement. There was no medical president to corroborate the nature of the existence of life. He had also spied, from a distance, men being shot by the Hunters after being paid for two rounds: in the head and in the heart. Derek reflexively found that his mother was still breathing, even though she had no pulse.

He began to check on every potential site he could think of, finally giving up knowing that he wasn't a good enough medical professional to assess what he didn't understand. Life was upside down.

"She won't move. I am not sure that she can move either. Derek, we can't do anything for her. You need to come with me!" she pleaded but to little avail.

Over the next several days, Derek tried to nurse his mom back to a semblance of health without the evidence of health. Derek could not do anything for the health of the ranch in his physical state. Tarra began to manage what she could within her limited understanding of all that needed to be done around their residence. Some of the chores were too demanding for her body to undertake, and they were left undone.

CHAPTER THIRTEEN

After about a month, Tarra was healing from her sting. All the while Derek had no idea how she was recovering so well, when no one in the world seemed to be having any success. He had not been stung, and his wound was healing with a little debriding service from Tarra. The only way Derek could handle the agony was to drink copious amounts of alcohol beforehand, but nothing could reduce his anguish. Derek would scream through the towel he bit during Tarra's procedures, and those wails encouraged his mother's cries until they blended in a sick harmony that bled into Tarra's soul. On the second such event, she put earplugs in with only a slight improvement. But wails pierced any level of reduction or masking of the noises that emanated from the two. They were miserable, but somehow the pain was higher for Charlene.

Charlene was nearly incapacitated sitting in her rocker-recliner. They would wrangle her out of the chair from time to time to clean the urine that dried into the fabric and sponge bathe her, while she shivered during the torturous affair. Her ghastly wounds were not improving which confused the young couple who tried to search the internet for more medical clues. The TV media was completely silent during this time, probably due to their horror in the flesh.

Somehow, a few channels had 24/7 frightful flicks on rerun which were not even funny anymore to Derek. The couple used to watch horror movies, and they both loved the thrill of excitement in their terror until the last couple of years. The realistic portrayals played out in HD contained too much graphic pragmatism for the already Post-Traumatic Stress Disordered citizens of the world. The media would gloat about the hangings, crucifixions and torturous beatings of Christians and Jews, who were belittled and humiliated in any possible means to reduce their humanity to that of lab rats to be disposed of once their entertainment value quotient was met.

Those *Google* searches became macabre depictions of murders and suicides that all horrifically failed. No matter if the victim were beheaded, the body would wander aimlessly until it fell still twitching. The eyes of the decapitated head were wide awake through the hellish display of portent endings of their world, and continued to do so even after the disgusting display except for those Christians. They seemed to die to the amazement of the announcers on the screen.

No one had answers, except for the two kooky Preachers standing by the Wailing Wall in Jerusalem, only minutes away from the Temple. The Two complained to the planet of the most disgusting displays of brutality and bestiality known to man by the Supreme Cartiff and his cronies. The world was circling the drain, and hope was lost except for Tarra.

She communicated regularly with her new-found saviors, as Derek termed them, only three miles up the road, Dr. Tony and Heather. They were supposedly training her up for the realities ahead that were worse than what the citizens were experiencing presently. Tarra had a lightness in her step and a song on her lips. Unfortunately for Derek, it was the same stupid few songs over and over again.

She called them *worship songs*, but all he wanted to do was strangle her when she belted her version of them, off-key, along with the tunes from her Galaxy S14 phone with a mounted Bluetooth speaker that pumped the infernal music into her workspace. He had to admit that she was more attractive daily as she recovered so quickly. Her demeanor was too pleasant for the skeptical mind of Derek in his time of lessening pain.

"Would you please come with me today, so that you can hear from Dr. Tony? I have already taken away your excuse, because I have redressed your mom and given her daily dropper dose of water. A lotta good that does her, because she spits it up. She hasn't taken any sustenance in weeks now. I know this is supposed to last for five months, but I cannot fathom how survival occurs for people like your mom, not just to mention now, but after the curse of the Zombie Trumpet is lifted, as Dr. Tony calls it," she slightly bemoaned with a pouty lip that he found adorable. He knew she was flirting with him to get him to accompany her. "Oh, they have some butter too. You'd like that on your eggs, wouldn't you? Or your potatoes?"

"Maybe the taters," Derek shrugged in final acceptance of her millionth proposal. He had wished for a little romantic interlude with her, now that he was feeling up to a bit of hanky panky as husband and wife, but he knew that he had to give to get. He picked up the keys to the Subaru sedan, the only vehicle which was working at the moment with the truck on the fritz and neither of them knew how to fix it.

The internet was surprisingly spotty on YouTube. The videos would not play, as if the servers were down for repair, which Derek realized could easily be the case since no one was able to work. All services, for that matter, were indefinitely suspended as the modern world became downright medieval in practice and culture. All were isolated from one another without regular shipping and media content to connect the world.

Derek pulled the car around in the back, and they pumped their gas from the massive reserves that Kenny had stored up a little at a time over the years. But even with the outdoor tanks that lined up with straw around them to shield them from view, they were running low and both of them were more aware of that fact each day. They filled up nonetheless, so that they didn't have to repeat the chore too many times due to the noxious nature of the fumes that didn't breathe off of the tanks well enough. She signaled for Derek to turn left to move farther away from the city of Boulder on Sunshine Canyon Drive toward the relative unknown as far as Derek was concerned. They rarely traversed in that direction unless they were thinking of hitting Bighorn Mountain. Almost as quickly as they had loaded up the car with the gas, they were pulling into Dr. Tony and Heather's driveway. Their slope had a steeper grade than the Ranch that the late Kenny had built.

Dr. Tony had his hand underneath his belt, in a posture of *shoot to kill*, until he recognized Tarra's car and released the death grip from behind him. He waved in the friendliest response Derek had seen in years, which brought a wry smile to his lips, that hadn't plastered one a month since the Zombie Trumpet had hit the planet. They completed the obligatory introductions, as well as a few niceties, until the host family got down to the depth of their conversation in what seemed to ramp up to warp six.

"Derek, I know you don't believe in any of this stuff about God's eternal plan, but would you at least hear me out?" Dr. Tony, after he was provided the nod from Derek to proceed, laid out the plan of salvation in the Gospels. The passion with which the man spoke, in his British eloquence, was refreshing and inviting since Derek loved accents but couldn't articulate the lilting of the proper British pronunciations. Tarra flitted about the two to serve him in a way that his common-law wife had never really done before. She then hid out in the kitchen, and the two women laughed softly at jokes that were not for Derek's consumption.

Dr. Tony recounted the life of Jesus and his research upon the death of the man for whom, he had supposed, was the Messiah that the Jews had been waiting for. He also gave the convincing evidence that Jesus had died with plasma separating in the Pericardial Sac of the heart almost nineteen hundred years before it was discovered by Dr. Charles Drew. It seemed that Tony knew that this kind of hard factual logic would appeal to the budding scientist's mind of Derek. Derek was hooked and losing control of his ability to contradict the nature of the religious beliefs that the man intimated, but one bastion held firm.

CHAPTER FOURTEEN

"Why did God take my dad when I was a kid?" Derek blurted with a crackle in his voice, and a tear staining his cheek. He was instantly embarrassed by the outburst that he didn't even know was going to blossom toward a man he didn't know.

"Great question, Derek," Dr. Tony appropriately held his hand upon Derek's left knee. "Did you know that God has been crying each time He thinks of you?"

"What? You serious? How can you know that pile of rubbish?" Derek unconsciously pulled a word from Tony's country of origin.

"Because the heart of God is deep. He cried when His own Son died on the Cross, on our behalf, as I explained to you. He knows the pain that the world loves to pile upon each of us. While I don't have a specific reason for the moment of your dad's departure from this earth, I can say with certainly it's the Devil's will to kill, steal and destroy, not God's."

"Ooookay," he elongated the retort that he needed time to dredge up. "Then if He is so powerful, why wouldn't He stop and kick Satan's butt out of my life?"

"Because the Father set up the rules of the universe that we live in mortal bodies upon the planet. These are the physical laws of the universe. Every once in a while, He reaches down to hijack those laws of the earth, so that a unique work can be done. But He certainly didn't stop the killing of His own Son, Jesus. Don't you think that He might have loved Jesus, a tad more than you loved your dad?"

"Guess so," Derek conceded.

"While we can blame God for all the bad things upon the earth, I lay the blame on a few separate areas. One, with Satan who loves to kill humanity; two, with my own choices that sometimes get me in massive trouble; three, with the world's other people who make choices which impinge upon my own life; and four, the natural causes of incidents in the world. Those could be murder, or much of the crimes humanity perpetrates upon itself. Which one of those would apply in this case? Could it be Satan or something of the world? Don't know which. But if we lay the blame at God's feet because we demand that He take some, and I think He would if we would..." Tony wanted to resolve the thought but saw that Derek needed to interject his questions.

"Whaddaya mean? *I* need to take the blame for my dad's death? *I* was a kid. *I* didn't do anything!" Derek was suddenly on his feet in strong defense of his past hurts with which he fervently protected.

"*I* didn't say you *did* anything regarding your dad's death. I *said* that if you would take the blame for your problems, I think that God would work with you about the other points of responsibility which you believe are His. Why don't we start with our own, or better yet my own?

Dr. Tony seemed to trail off, lost in thought. He explained that he lost his dad when he was nineteen, while he had been off at college in Cambridge for Pre-Med. Dr. Tony didn't even have the time to make it to his father's funeral. He revealed that he hated God for what He did to Tony. But his first wife had pleaded with Tony to accept Jesus from the moment that he was forty until five years earlier.

"What happened to her? Did she divorce you?" Derek winced only seconds after making the silly conclusion without knowing the facts.

"She should have. I was a piece of work, as you Yankees like to say. I moved here when we met in med school, when she was a graduate exchange student in London. I fell for that beauty in an instant and was hooked. Once we had our first child, and I was in my residency, I had little time for a family. I was hoping that she would put her Biology research on hold for my needs. She did so, begrudgingly, at the time.

"Somehow, my wife had learned of a church, from a playgroup mom, when our son was three years old, because she needed a little adult time without me around." Tony went on to explain that the two moved to Denver for Tony's first attending position at St. Joe's. He wanted to research with the best in lung replacement therapies and was only focused on his next case that would propel his career forward. He began to note that he had stopped counting at one hundred-hour weeks, not to mention the female pharmaceutical reps who came in his office with their business hanging out. A pained expression played over Dr. Tony's features, as he recounted a life that Derek would have killed for. Women, wine and work were the three W's that would have sustained him to greatness in medicine.

"So, you were sowing your wild oats? *Bravo, doctor!*" the last phrase uttered in a whisper. "As long as no one knew it!" Another murmur from Derek. So far, he was impressed with this fiftyish man's resume. The Physician was greying along his temples but was ruggedly handsome in a way that Derek would have hoped his father would have been. As Derek admired the work and career of his newest mentor in, *how to survive, then thrive, when the world calms from this warring state*, the older man looked back at him displeased.

"Derek, you just don't get it! Those are my *faults*; they are not my moments of pride," a stern-faced Dr. Tony peered back at Derek down from his glasses. At this point, Derek wanted to crawl into a hole for the night. He had misunderstood the direction of the conversation so thoroughly that he lost sight of the point of the story.

"Uh...uh...I mean...can I use the restroom?" Derek begged off and rose quickly to where Dr. Tony referred was the direction of their downstairs bathroom.

"How's it going in here?" the two women came in as soon as they heard the bathroom door close.

"He's not getting it. He thinks my past sins with Kelly, and the many women I slept with while I was a younger attending, were a good thing," Dr. Tony complained as he held his head in his hands in confusion as to a new direction for his plea for Derek's soul. The women gathered around to place their hands upon the head of Dr. Tony to pray for his guidance in speaking the truth to Derek.

His new beautiful redheaded wife, Heather, quietly prayed a fantastic prayer that brought tears to Tarra. Tarra was such a new *Called* Saint, as the Two Witnesses denoted believers in this turbulent time, which she didn't yet know the right words to speak in any eloquence to the Lord. But as Heather motioned for Tarra to pray, she let go and spoke the words that were in her spirit but were not yet in her soul.

"We need the wisdom of the ages to impart truth to Derek, so that he may be convinced by your verification techniques inside of the Word. We are such a stubborn people, even more so than anyone spoken of in the Book. Forgive all of us for being so critically and willfully blind. We want you, Jesus," Tarra opened her eyes, and the couple looked up with tears in their eyes at the wisdom that parted the lips of the young woman, no more than one month in the Lord.

Tony and Heather had poured over the Scriptures for the past year, non-stop, but they knew that those behind them, already Raptured, had the understanding of dozens of years of study that they didn't have. There was a sense that God was accelerating the download process, in the stormy times, faster than they could pluck off a Word document from their emails. Understanding as to where to read, and what to say came forth from their lips without the full ability to process the wisdom. It made them feel like a tool of the King to impart His brain through their vocal processing.

But when Derek entered the room, seeing the closeness that existed between the three people who were perceptibly on the opposite side of the Grace fence than he was, the conversation seemed to be tacitly over. The whole gaggle knew it. Derek, to his credit, didn't signal that he was going to be a poor guest by pleading his way out of a filling meal that was brewing in the kitchen. "I am famished. Could we break for the kitchen table?" Derek asked as he raised his hand in acknowledgment of a terminating event to their prayer.

They ate with an awkward silence as the three allowed Derek to process what Dr. Tony had revealed about his life. His eyes seemed to be distant. All were polite, trying to create new conversations that were banal enough not to offend Derek into leaving the couple's home in anger. All were balancing with the fact that they lived in such a dangerous time that death was around the bend after the five months would end, approximately one hundred days later.

CHAPTER FIFTEEN

"Can I ask you something?" Derek asked, changing the subject from the trivial, as they munched upon a few veggies.

"Shoot!" Dr. Tony retorted without thinking which brought a cringe-worthy crunching of the eyes from his wife, Heather. Gun violence was so prevalent that the phrase had an open frivolity that they didn't want to entertain anymore. Dr. Tony didn't see the expression of his wife, even though Tarra noted Heather's reaction for future reference with her two new friends.

"What's happening in the world now, at least from your religious view? I mean, I need to take into account all sides of the story: secular and sacred," Derek explained as if he were a journalist attempting to frame his question in neutrality.

Taking no offense to the potential insult of the question, Dr. Tony launched in. "Well, the Bible doesn't always give us the *hows* and *whens* in reference to the End Times."

"You mean the apocalypse ending we may or may not be living through? But there has to be an end to it all, so that the world can rebuild, correct? Post-apocalyptic stories indicate a big event in which most of the people die, except those who are prepared to outlast the craziness of the time. I intend to outlast it and become a doctor like you, Dr. Tony. Maybe, you can teach me your profession along with my studies. We will need trained medical professionals in the new days of rebuilding," Derek offered.

"I think you misunderstand what the Bible is saying. Did you know that the apocalypse that the world thinks of as a huge set of events ending this cultural time period of the world is the opposite of what the Word actually says?" Dr. Tony redirected the answer with his question to focus Derek's thoughts. The four began in the light main course of the meal.

"Nah, didn't know that," he forked more chicken in his mouth awkwardly with his left hand. Tarra had helped by cutting the chicken for him on his plate without the use of his right dominant hand.

"The Bible calls this *the Tribulation* in which is apportioned seven years of trouble. The Two Witnesses layout the Scriptures so eloquently. I have searched the Bible verses, so that I can figure out what they are saying. You see the Bible does tell us the *whys*," Dr. Tony explained his hands gesticulating to make his point.

"So why don't you believe that the world is ending?" Tarra asked, not just for Derek, but because she needed the answer. "The facts of the end are all around us."

"Oh, don't get me wrong. It is ending. Just not the way that the movies portray it. They lie. It's the trick of Satan inside of that beast in the palace!" Dr. Tony pointed off toward the TV with such a vehemence that Tarra recoiled a bit. "He is the god of the air, and the director of this moment in time that's probably about two years away from its conclusion. Did you know that the movies are half right though?"

"In what way?" Derek continued with the points Dr. Tony was making.

"If the days aren't ended, all flesh would die, as the book of Matthew says. That's different than any of those apocalyptic movies indicate. All life would cease. *That's* the Devil's real aim. He wants to kill us all, first the Jews, Jesus' Remnant, then we Called Saints, then the rest of the world who hasn't claimed their damnable Marker. But we are living in the last three and half years in which hell is literally turned loose upon the earth. Most people feel that God is wringing out His wrath upon the planet right now. But, that's not exactly how the Two Witnesses are putting it.

"God is allowing Satan to push all of the people of the earth to join him in one last bid for his scorching eternity, because he knows it is coming soon. This timeframe is to get people off the fence with God and choose. It's about *you* most of all!" Dr. Tony ended with a flourish.

"Me? What does the world want with me in their cosmic game against one another as you put it?" Derek was taken aback by the comment, even if his hubris was puffed up a little bit.

"You haven't made a choice for or against Christ. The Devil knows it and is coming for all those who don't have a seal of God on their forehead with every trick in the book. I could not be harmed by the creatures that bit Tarra. They were not allowed to create a pain on me. They are the reason that your mother has tried to kill herself so many times. The chat rooms are calling the unsuccessful tries as *zombifying,* you know?"

"Yeah, I do. How can she fix her suffering?" Derek beseeched for his mother's death in an odd reversal of the Hippocratic Oath that Derek hadn't pled yet for his chosen future profession.

"There's nothing that will end it other than what I think will happen in 100 days," Dr. Tony dipped his head in resignation and dug into his plate in a vain hope that Derek would change the subject, even though he knew it was impossible for the young man to do.

"Come on, you won't even try? Aren't you a doctor who wants to help people?" Derek bemoaned as he bounced his fork off of his plate that clanged louder than he had wanted it to for his host's dishes. Derek's passion was displaying his compassion that Dr. Tony had lost for his patients. "Sorry, thank you for the meal, but I have to get back to tending to my mother. I appreciate the hospitality...both of you. The food was excellent, but I have responsibilities," Derek rose from the table to pick up his plate, but Heather wouldn't have him cleaning the dishes with one hand.

"Please, talk to us a little longer?" Heather laid her hand upon Derek's right elbow above his amputation with a gentle touch. But that remembrance of his wound only served to resolve his course of action to leave the couple to their own devices.

"Thank you very much. Come on Tarra, we need to go," Derek was already heading for the door looking for his coat as autumn had hit in full force with a wind coming from the Rocky Mountains. The nights would be biting on the stump of Derek without more pain pills.

He had alternatively been using alcohol to abate the agony that was only waning a little over the weeks since his amputation. He didn't want to be another drug addict statistic, even though he feared that he might have a dualistic addiction to both drugs and alcohol, which he would announce to an AA meeting of the future: *Hi, my name is Dr. Derek Fultz and I am a drug and alcohol addict.*

Tarra apologized with her eyes in silent resignation due to their sudden departure. Dr.

Tony barely looked up, with a tear in his eye, knowing that he was choking on his failure with Derek. Heather, for her part of the soundless conversation, indicated that all would be alright in their household and that, with a nod, Tarra was going to have a tougher time than the sadness that Tony was displaying.

The two young lovers, having been married in a very private ceremony, in Charlene's property called the Ranch, only a year ago, drove home with no conversations. The only sound was the gear shifts of the old, three hundred thousand mile Subaru that Kenny wanted for their safety from the government's prying eyes. Derek reached out to Tarra with his left hand which still had the wedding ring of brass they had procured for one another on his ring finger. He placed his hand upon her leg in acceptance of who she was in his life. She patted his hand but could not leave her hand on top of his to shift her way home the three-mile trip.

CHAPTER SIXTEEN

Another month passed at the Ranch with no healing in sight for Charlene. The Zombie Trumpet nightmare reappeared in Boulder. The rest of the planet also experienced the wave of horrid bites when the demons screamed their epithets saying *the Zombie Trumpet*. Amazingly for Derek, the words were instantly translated into the language of the hearer, which he could not reconcile how it was happening. New video evidence, that didn't occur on the first appearance of the stings, showed that those infected again with the Zombie Plague were redoubled in their pain if that were at all possible.

Those who hadn't been stung in the past were found by the demon personalities which had odd semblances: the hair and faces were similar to the hippy movement of the 1960s in which men loved the long-tangled hair and unkempt beards. They had golden crowns on their heads to signify their position over the humans on the planet. The demons threatened this time that if the god of the air was not worshipped they would bite with a worse sting than before.

Those suffering were also told that their torment would last for an eternity that the agonized instantly believed. Almost all bowed their heads, in some form of adoration, to the godhead triumphant in the palaces of the plains of the Middle East, consisting of Supreme Governor Cartiff, and his religious leader who dropped his original title to go by the name of *The Messiah of the Universe.* The role of the messiah was to direct the worship of the faithless of the globe toward their leader and god: the Supreme Cartiff.

The rouse was played out on smartphone videos posted to the web with the high-speed highway that was working again. It seemed that Cartiff's people had restored internet service by the servers that were rolled out supposedly prepared for this time. It was as if the world government had foreseen the stalling of basic amenities of humanity, specifically of the communication grid to recreate it again. Once the supplicant bowed toward the east, then the demon laughed as it stung them anew.

The oddity, as far as Derek was concerned, was the nature of the Two Witnesses. It seemed to be one of the only websites that were fully functional during the loss of services throughout the globe. The site allowed the Saints, such as Tarra, to upload videos of the deception by the demons. But they also recorded how the Sealed of God repelled the demons as they came upon them. The Saints were not being harmed even once in any video. They were surrounded at times by the Zombie Horde of demons, but after recognizing that they could not sting the person with an impenetrable shield, they moved on, cursing them during their retreat.

Tarra passionately tried to engage Derek in monologues about how he needed Jesus. Alternatively, he listened or begged off of the pronouncements in his efforts to treat his mother. Derek noticed how eerie it was to care for his mother. She hadn't spoken in weeks, other than primal grunts of pain with ragged breaths. She would sleep for a few minutes and then moan for a few minutes. Charlene's existence was a never-ending torture chamber within her favorite chair. She began to rebel each time they tried to move her from her throne. In surrender, they sprayed air freshener from behind her, due to the overpowering odor that arose from Charlene.

"Have you noticed her breathing pattern?" Derek teared up when staring at his mom, while Tarra cleaned through the living room. They had moved her rocker closer to the window which calmed her somewhat, but it also had the secondary effect of distancing her powerful stink from the family room.

"Yeah," she stood ten feet away. "She's dying. It's so slow that it's difficult to completely recognize the overt physical signs, but they are there." Tarra placed her hand upon the uninjured elbow of her man as she passed by not speaking the rest of the sentence. She had also realized that Derek was slowing down as well. He had much less energy each day. She was worried that he could be next on the platform of a slow death unless there were a spirit change.

"No one dies in this Zombie time!" he retorted back a little too angrily. "But *she* is getting worse," he admitted to the diagnostic skills that she obtained by watching his patient. Derek sat on the edge of the couch fifteen feet away out of the fire of her odor and in range of essential oils that were being diffused in the house. The scents were more pleasant than he was. The comparison between the rank nature of his mother, as related to his own, was only apparent when he was not downwind of Charlene.

As the cold of autumn seeped into Boulder, the heater flowed only at certain times of the day to preserve gasoline that was the only thing that ran their furnace. They could run the unit maybe an hour a day to increase the internal temperature in the morning. The rest of the day needed a fire to blaze inside to ward off the cold that had dipped a week after Halloween.

Halloween. No one celebrated Halloween anymore, especially not with the nature of the wounds available along the Rocky Mountains. In his endless reverie, which was the only thing that sustained him, he was awoken by a demon while Tarra was outside in the barn.

"Bow to the lord of the earth!" the demon with a booming voice that belied his lack of size when he demanded compliance. "Pray that I will leave you be!"

"Tar...Ta..." white with fear, Derek came face to face with his doom. He couldn't move a muscle and was stuttering unable to communicate his needs. The creature began to curse him and speak of how his father had died. He conjured notions in the mind that his father was a weakling at the point of his death. Derek began to shudder. He was unprepared for the rantings of a being who knew all there was to know about what scared him.

"Get out of here you Zombie demon! IN JESUS' NAME!" Tarra screamed from the back door with an intensity that startled both Derek, and the creature for a moment. The panic was short-lived in the scorpion as it stung Derek in the left arm as he bolted through the open door. Derek reflexively yelped in pain, holding his left shoulder with his right stump. Derek lay upon the wood flooring just inside the outer door for what felt like hours without relief. At first, other wounds hurt on the top end of the tolerance scale but reduced into pulsing of distress. His new torture didn't change after minutes or even hours later. He writhed, prone in agony, unable to think. He finally understood what the world had been experiencing from the infernal creatures sent to torture the people.

During the next four days, the pain was too great to bear. On the fifth day, he had made a fateful decision at four AM. He was convinced that he could end his suffering. Derek pulled a pen out to write a note to his beloved wife.

As stealthily as possible, Derek crept out onto the back porch. He slipped his pants down and found the femoral artery in both legs and sliced them expertly, with significant force, to bleed like a stuck pig. The spurting made it challenging to pull up his jeans, but his efforts were rewarded seconds later. He hoped that even if Tarra could find him and bandage him up in time, his skinny jeans would make it difficult to get to the wounds. All of his blood would flow from his veins. He was feeling the two cuts almost at the same angst as the sting in his left arm. Surprisingly, he didn't have as much of his fluids exuding from his wounds as he had believed.

He awaited death to release him from his worthless existence. When his vision blurred on the sides, he believed that he would be successful where others were not. An odd smile came to his lips, knowing that his suffering would cease in a couple more minutes. His legs were soaked in blood that stained everything from his knees down in the acrid scent that life-giving liquid emanated. After ten minutes of sitting in his pool of life dripping from his body, he noticed a pasty hue from both of his forearms as he lay on his side, unable to sit straight upward. He blacked out as he felt that he was the only one in the world who was successful in achieving death.

CHAPTER SEVENTEEN

Tarra, when she first found Derek on the back porch, believed that he had accomplished what the Bible indicated was not possible for their current time. She had never seen that much blood, even with all the suffering around her. The deck was covered with a new wood stain which would probably stay that color for the rest of their time on the earth. Tarra had almost given up during her first days after the sting as well with all those around her sitting in the pools of their death. She felt led to check Derek's breathing and noted that he was still alive, which could not seem possible.

She stripped off his clothing and cleaned him up, outside of the smear of his blood. She sewed up the wounds and dragged him indoors, so that he could be near his mother on the couch. Tarra didn't know what to do with him to create life in him, but knew that with the Bible, all things were possible.

"Can you guys come over and help me? I don't know what to do for him anymore. He sliced himself open. I was healed of my sting from the Zombie demons; maybe he could be as well?" She spoke into her Galaxy S14 in tears.

"We'll be over there as soon as Tony gets home," Heather promised. Once he arrived, she apprised him of the situation as it was explained to her. Dr. Tony hung his head in near despair.

"Do all my prayers go unanswered? I have been so on that boy! I have only had a few kids to talk to, and he would be my first to accept the Lord!" Tony complained to his wife in tears, knowing that being unsuccessful was like killing one of his patients who were healthy in the Operating Room.

"It's not your job, Doctor. It's Dr. Jesus who saves, not you," Heather always had a way of correcting his thought processes in the most gentle, but firm manner. He reached up to brush away the gorgeous straight hair from the scar that she hid, a result of being beaten last year by marauding Hunters who tried to take her for sport. Tony had hurled curse words and Jesus' name in the same sentences, blowing his record for not cussing that week. The Hunters, so off guard by hearing the curses and the name of Jesus concurrently began to laugh, until they fell on the ground dead in front of the couple. There was no explicable reason for sudden deaths. Heather moved away at lightning speed. Then he realized that God wasn't offended at the curse words, but Tony wanted to act in a manner that Jesus would have while on earth.

The couple drove and prayed on the way to Tarra's abode. The Holy Spirit gave them a hint; it would be a marathon event in the house.

Heather pushed open the door. She knew it would be fine for her to walk in unannounced imagining that Tarra would have her hands full with two dying people, and no time to herself or for the Ranch. Tarra allowed Heather to pull her away from caring for the two, as she set her on her bed to nap. The friendly intruders were on duty.

Heather flitted about the house looking for a way to clean the kitchen or create enough food to sustain the cadre for several days. She didn't slow down for almost four hours. Heather felt more energized as she was Spirit directed throughout the house and the Ranch for the preparation needed.

Tony bee-lined to Charlene to assess her physical status. It took him a moment to compose himself since it had been years since he had whiffed that deathly kind of odor. After a few seconds, he realized that there was nothing to do. He didn't know when or if she would die for sure due to the strangest time in human history for a physician's skills, but he knew there wasn't anything to do with her near rigor mortis repose on her recliner.

Dr. Tony gently tapped at the younger man's cheek to try to revive him and spoke in hushed tones. When Derek opened his eyes, he was extremely unfocused, as a small baby might be, trying to see what was out of focus. Tony then began to snap and attempted to gain Derek's attention by asking him to look at his pointer finger. When he was successful, he began his resuscitation.

"I know you were trying to die son, but the Will of God has its time to perfect what we cannot."

"What are you talking about, old man?" Derek wiped at his forehead as if he could shoo Dr. Tony away as he would a fly.

"God won't let you die right yet. I am here so that you can hear of the life plan God has for you. Would you please listen?" Tony spoke with such emotion in the last question that it fixated Derek upon what the older man was saying. Derek nodded his ascension.

"Jesus wants you for the kingdom. You are not going to get the martyr's crown, but you can get in with your shorts intact," he was trying a form of downhome insight that he had heard other country doctors use, but his was with a heavy English accent. Without the Southern drawl, it didn't have the same effect.

"Wasn't aiming for your crown, grey beard," Derek joked at the salt and pepper that speckled Tony's fur on his face, since the last time he had seen him about six weeks prior. "But I am trying to create a march toward eternity."

"Let me read you a couple of verses that might be your lot," Tony pulled out his phone and used the iPhone app for an Olive Tree Study Bible he had heard about with the HCSB version available. "I Corinthians 3:13-15 says, '...each one's work will become obvious, for the day will disclose it, because it will be revealed by fire: the first will test the quality of each one's work. If anyone's work that he has built survives, he will receive a reward. If anyone's work is burned up, it will be lost, but he will be saved; yet it will be like an escape through fire.'"

"So, I need fire insurance?" Tony was surprised by the lucidity of the jokes from a very sickly man.

"And I'm the insurance salesman," Tony quipped back.

"What does it mean though?" Derek settled his chin in to listen for the first time to the meaning of a Bible verse. There was a relevance that this older man brought to an ancient book that Derek never considered before facing his death.

"It's not talking about the work that one might do to please God. There is nothing that we can do to please the One who made us by our works outside of God."

"Then He hates us?"

"Well, yes, in the lie that our sin which permeates this life, and our unacceptance of the Son to remove that sin, you might say that the Father does. But the *Day* that the Word is discussing is a layered semantic. Partly, we see that it is talking about the judgment day of

Christ, which I think is about fourteen months away from now. But it is also dualistic in its semantic to entail your end."

"American English, you Brit," Derek complained.

"Uh, let me think of another way to say it," Tony rose to his feet, knowing that he thought better on his toes. "There are always tests in life. ACTs to get into college, MCATS and Doctoral Dissertations that have to be passed. Then, I had my board exams and so on. Those get us from one step to another. But this whole life is a test, and it's so easy that a moron like yourself can even pass it," Tony smiled down knowing that the boy would catch his drift. A smile and a slight nod were passed back to Tony with a grimace of his whole body being racked with pain. "OK, so think of it this way: from the beginning of the universe, Jesus knew our every step. I know that sounds crazy to you, but He's God, and we are not. He sees it all, my young friend."

"OK, let's say that I grant you that one. And, let's say He does see it all. He's gotta see that I tried to devote my life to the preservation of life and never raped or killed anyone. I am a good person," Derek complained.

"Are you perfect?"

"No, but who is?" Derek countered.

"Jesus. The rules of the Monopoly game are set up in a particular way. For God's game board, this life in which we live, He gets to play it any way He wishes. You heard about House Rules?" Tony queried.

"Sure, I like your Monopoly reference, cuz you're not getting my green land unless you give me something massive in return."

"That's the spirit. It's your rules when I come over. But we live in the creation of the Father. He created the rules of the game. In His scenario, if a person does *anything* wrong, he is called a rulebreaker. Have you ever lied, stolen, cheated, or done anything that you think could be considered a sin in the Bible?" Tony cocked his eyebrow, pushing Derek to be honest.

"'Course I have, but that's a pretty tall order to say that I am a rule breaker."

"I had an English class in college before I was going to be a Physician. If you had one mechanical mistake it was a *D*. Two was an *F*. The professor was an old garbage man who got his Ph.D. later in life before teaching at Cambridge. He would put the works of Chaucer upon the chalkboard and indicated the grammatical mistakes the writer exuded in his sentence structures. We were shocked at the nature of the measuring stick; us against the greatest writers of all time! But those were his rules to pass the class. By the way, I got a *D* in the class," both chuckled a bit until Derek coughed in obvious pain. "But, those were the rules of the class. Does it feel fair? Can we complain about it? Sure, we could but Jesus gives you an easy *A*. Want to know how?"

"Gotta hear this one," Derek replied.

"He already took the test for you, or you could say that he played the Monopoly game and won it for you! You have to accept that He did that for you and love the One who did. I think those are the easiest rules I have ever heard about. Don't you?" Tony beamed.

"Gotta be a catch?"

"Well, there is at that. You have to accept that *you* cannot keep the rules. The rules were only there to show you that you needed someone else to play the Game of Life for you. Let Him play that game, and read His own words to get to know Him. Do you want to do that?" Tony sat back on the other end of the couch waiting patiently for his reply, knowing that it might take Derek some time to process this new information that he may have never heard before. Tony could perceive in the spirit that he had his undivided attention and that the wheels were turning inside.

"If I do that, will God take away this curse of the sting bite as He did with Tarra?" It was Tony's turn to ponder that one for a moment, but the answer came to him in a flash of inspiration.

"If I said yes, you would be motivated to do it, because you were gaining something in the here and now. If I said no, you might be mad at God for not caring, even when you would be putting yourself out there on a limb for Him. The answer is that I do not know. I don't know if God will heal you instantly or not. But that's not the point."

"What *is* the point then?"

Tony went on to bring a piece of paper to diagram the parts of the body, soul, and spirit, so that Derek could comprehend the place that each had within the life of the human. He already knew that his body was dying, but Derek needed to realize that his spirit was already dead.

The crux of the concept was that Derek needed a new spirit for the next chapter of his life, whether he survived this moment or not. Derek then began to understand that his life was more meaningless than ever. He had existed upon this planet for his purposes, and he could search below his neck to find the fruits of that decision: death. He had longed to die. He had heard of a Hell and asked about this with Tony who schooled him upon the permanence of Hades.

"You are living in a time, Derek, when God has allowed Hell to invade the earth. Don't you already feel that?" Tony pleaded with all of his senses trying to reach this young man who unexpectedly leaked from his eyes.

"I see that now. I don't want an eternity of this torture. I really want to be free of *me*, this body, and who I am. How do I do that?" Derek was never more serious than at that moment to put his selfish desires aside. Almost as if it were on cue, the women came into the room, and Tony beckoned them over, with the permission of Derek, to enter their private conversation. Derek didn't care anymore about his pride.

Derek started to drip tears of pain and joy, along with remorse that confused his senses, until he could not bodily feel the difference between his emotions. He allowed his dendrites to shut off their neural firing, almost subconsciously. He began to feel a heavenly lifting of his condition, until the agony he had experienced since he was bitten disappeared.

The sins of his life feel like banana peels wasting away in the trash. He lost track of what he was confessing. Derek flashed his brown eyes upward, expecting that their disgust for his inner sinfulness would be too repelling for these wholesome people to handle. Instead, he was unhinged to learn that they cried for joy and raised their hands in praise to their Father above, who was suddenly his Father. That response created a more enormous outpouring of his soul in confession of who he wasn't. He understood what God could be in him, as Derek couldn't even recognize his language anymore.

The young man was startled to hear himself sputter unintelligible words from his lips that had no meaning. He pieced sentences and whole phraseologies into passages of a language he didn't know as Tony held Derek's hand to stop him.

"What'd I say?" Derek stopped as if he had offended his new brother in Christ.

With choking sobs, Tony knelt down, grabbing the younger man's knees. Both faces were a blur of tears that made them unrecognizable to one another through their haze of emotions. "You spoke the prayer of my grandmother who was Hungarian. She used to repeat it to me each night. 'Love came to die; love came to kill that which was useless. I desire that love; I will live for that love inside of Jesus.'"

"I have heard you tell me those sentences before, honey," Heather laid her hand upon the sweaty hair of the man of her life, consumed by Dr. Tony's emotions, giving in to the Spirit making him the most desirous human on the planet in her eyes.

CHAPTER EIGHTEEN

Derek had given his heart to Jesus, but his pain decreased only a little, when he listened to the Word from a set of CDs that were playing night and day. He used his remote to cut the sound every few songs, while he learned to look up the Scripture references within the amazing worship sets. The Bible was so different than standard studies of texts. One could look up a chapter that could be dozens of pages long; on the other hand, many of the books of the Bible were more of the length of a medical section. Derek mentally compared the chapters of the Bible to subheadings.

Tarra busily moved about the house, trying to accomplish the needs of the Ranch, so that the three of them might have their daily bread. Derek would eat less than a few hundred calories a day, saying that each time he ate more, he wanted to puke his guts up. He had precious little energy, and what he had was expended upon the nature of his studies. Tarra loved that Derek would repeat, with great verbal vigor, the nuances of verses he was discovering. He never talked about sex anymore; something he obsessed with beforehand which made her self-conscious. When she would broach the topic, wondering if she was unattractive to him, he had an opposite comment.

"I am more in love with my wife right now than I ever was before. I want to make myself into the man who can be the *Leader of the Band*, as Dan Fogelberg sang about. I heard that when the Apostle Harry, I think it is, described in Ephesians that I was a Bride. I am not sure if I am, because it is pretty girly to me. But if my Jesus says so, I will be that for you. I'm not going to cross-dress though," Derek looked so severe when he made his proclamations that Tarra had to turn her head in laughter. She had learned a little more about what she thought her man was describing.

"Don't you mean Jamie who wrote Ephesians?" she queried, knowing that she might be wrong herself.

"Whichever dude said it, God says that He says it. Doesn't matter. But I am not that comfortable with the concept of being a Bride. To answer your question, I actually respect you more now that I came into these Bible *books* and *subheadings*. You are my love on this earth, but they are so *butter* for me. I can't get enough of it..." he wandered back into the Word again.

A knock that clattered against the door with a brush indicated that Dr. Tony and Heather were coming over. They let themselves in, knowing that the last month the two couples were the parchment to each other's souls. Tony and Derek would debate and research the Scriptures together, while the two women created the atmosphere about the men in service. Heather wasn't trying to regress in time as a servant, which she hated to be when she was married to a man who wouldn't lift a finger after work. Her new Physician husband was a dream come true, and she found her passion was to be his helpmate, as she read within her Bible.

Tony tried to check in on Charlene who was worse each moment. Sometimes, she seemed to be in a coma barely breathing; then in the next second, she would lash out at him with a backhand and the "F" word for his troubles. Most words uttered from her lips, with curses and demonic statements, were meant to harm the burgeoning spirits that were growing in the room around the dying elder. A demon or two had attached themselves to her being, but Tony's commands *to drip them in the blood of Christ* shut her up, outside of inaudible mutterings that would not cease. All of the souls in the house jumped when the TV blared to life upon the World News Channel which was a mosh pit of the old Fox/CNN/MSNBC broadcast teams.

"I did not have that on!" Derek shouted over the sudden din of TV noise.

"I was reading that when they wish to push their broadcasts, they can turn all TV's on at will. You can mute it, but the closed captioning will flash up on the screen. Smart TV's have been connected to the network systems for many years for this purpose. We unhooked ours with great effort," Heather reported.

"Could you guys fix ours as well? Used to like it connected, because it gave me info on the man in charge whom I respected. Now, I know him as the Anti-Christ!" Tarra stated. When his ancient title was used, Charlene stirred from her stupor and focused intently upon the TV. She uttered praises to the man to whom she was pledging her existence.

"My mom never used to say that kind of stuff," Derek cocked his eyebrow at her.

"It's not her anymore. Your mother has left this reality, and it's her dead spirit woman who is preaching that message. Did you know that the Gospel writers mentioned that one could be either for Him or against Him, not in-between? Many of my old studies of theologians didn't seem to grasp this fundamental fact that is evident within this world today. We completely understand it now, don't we?" Tony asked with the nodded ascent of the room.

The foursome did spend a little time watching what was being presented on the broadcast. A string of WNN experts came on the screen in a panel of death. American Hunter managers in the old USA were seated along with two physicians who sat before the camera. The makeup artists were working overtime to create the image of a transsexual set of men with one woman. All were gaunt and even pasty. It seemed that they had no blood within at least three of the seven-panel members. The network tried to get the best faces available, but one of the men had a scar from ear to ear that was visible as he held his neck up, trying to keep his head in a vertical position. His neck muscles were too weak to move.

The loose necked man, introducing himself as Dr. Terrance, explained that he had cut himself trying to release his pain with many of the tendons and ligaments severed. He indicated a need for a permanent neck brace. Dr. Terrance had to hold his head very still as he talked which was difficult for a gregarious speaker to accomplish.

"We have identified the drug that was released into the general population called Tetrodotoxin," Dr. Terrance explained with his right fingers gently along his jowl line.

"Wait, what is that drug?" the mediator of the discussion seemed ill-prepared with the comment, and then he regained his composure.

"Thank you for asking that, James. It's loosely called *The Zombie Drug* that was made famous in the 1988 cult-classic, *Serpent and the Rainbow,*" Dr. Terrance began but was interrupted by the other guests.

"I loved that film growing up. It fed me!" a guest responded with vigor.

"Yes, and so did I. I have spent time researching those effects," Dr. Terrance added.

"Which are what exactly?" James, the mediator, pushed the questioning forward.

"Tetrodotoxin, in the correct dosages, creates a depressive state within the victim, making him or her susceptible to influences of the criminal administering the neurotoxin. The effect is a catatonic state which can create one who can do about anything, including killing oneself or creating other harmful acts upon the law-abiding citizens, loyal to the master of the universe, the Lord Cartiff..." Dr. Terrance trailed off.

The screen flashed an announcement that all must bow on their mats in front of them to worship their savior, Cartiff, for two minutes of adoration. All the attendees of the panel immediately posed prostrate for the camera. Even Dr. Terrance held his cranium with both hands as he performed the ritual. After the screen released the population from their solemn duty, they began to compose themselves back to their positions.

"Ah, yes....well...anyway...We believe that the Tetrodotoxin was weaponized by the White aliens, who work for the enemy Called Saints, as they refer to themselves. Those Whites stung us with this drug that was replicated at this captured facility in Billings, Montana, as the footage here shows," Dr. Terrance paused to allow the network to split-screen to a shot of federal agents and grey uniformed Hunters barging their way into a bunker.

In the facility, the people without the Marker were cobbling together powders that didn't look like drugs. It was obvious to the two couples watching that it was baking paraphernalia, whereas the onscreen experts openly reveled, with fists held high, each time a Hunter offed a suspect with blows to the head, using their machetes or nine MMS to the brains of their victims. After blood spurted about the facility which was deemed an enemy of the state of Cartiff, the powder upon the kitchen table was presented as evidence frozen upon the screen.

"You see I identified this powder in the raid of the Called Saints in their murderous rage against the peaceful people of this world as Tetrodotoxin," another guest who hadn't spoken yet piped up who was the healthiest looking one of the group.

"Yes, Dr. Bevil. Your expertise is in weapons and drugs. What a unique combination," the host James touched Dr. Bevil on his leg, in an almost sexual manner an overt flirtation with the male doctor. The rest of the guests stirred due to the chemistry that was being displayed on the screen. James left his hand upon the man's leg, while he leaned in to hear what the doctor was saying. The Physician, for his part, played along with the gesture by covering James' hand with his allowing it to rest there.

"I worked for the division of Alcohol, Tobacco and Firearms in the weaponized division. As you know my love," Dr. Bevil referred back to James. "After I received my medical degree and completed my residency in Georgia, I led the raid on the distribution center in our North American continental states which gave the Whites their base for killing off the legal population of this world. It was a rather ingenious plan to create Zombies who could not die but were in pain twenty-four-seven, as all of us on the panel can attest. Last week, though, they finally got me as well," Dr. Bevil motioned to his neck, where an angry welt bubbled up two inches high. "I am so glad that the population is healing now; that we are coming to the end of this terrible terror attack upon the people of the globe."

"How do you know that, Dr. Bevil?" James asked.

"Because we have determined that its effect can only last approximately six months. The chemical influence had been increased in potency seventeen times its dose. Even if you committed suicide or had one of our glorious Hunters contract kill you, you would not experience death. We don't know how they increased that drug to its chemical levels. We know through websites that are also on-screen, they aimed to kill billions so that they could have the planet again. We believe that the Saint's desire was to repopulate it with their degenerate, hateful religion of complete intolerance to the men and women of this great union, under my god, Cartiff," Dr. Bevil bowed his head.

"I can answer another portion of this mystery we solved," the only woman on the panel spoke up with her hand half raised.

"Yes, Dr. Michelle?" James allowed for the interruption.

"As you know from the frequent broadcasts, I am an epidemiologist as an expert in infectious diseases. I studied the chemical makeup of the compound in that daring raid, led by the courageous Dr. Bevil, who put his life at risk for the good of the people. Thank you for that!" Dr. Michelle and the others nodded to Dr. Bevil who also responded with a short acknowledgment.

"The long-lasting effects of the drug were implanted within the host in the most insidious nature by the White's claiming to be angels, which we know that they are, according to our Grey Hosts. Our Lord Cartiff has told us that the Greys have ushered us into world peace within a new one world religion of which we worship four times a day."

"We are all glad to join in that collective worship," James intoned.

"That doesn't even look like any medical type powder!" Derek complained to the TV.

"I know! It's probably baking soda with flour mixed into it, but the lies of the enemy will sound like truth to the foolish. I am reminded of a verse that talks about these days in Matthew 24:24: 'False messiahs and false prophets will arise and perform great signs and wonders to lead astray, if possible, even the elect.'"

"That sounds like us, doesn't it?" Tarra asked.

"Well it is, and it isn't. The Elect were the Chosen that were taken up in a Rapture in the middle of this terrible time. They had much more deception and didn't even believe in an end. All of us, though, who survived as preppers believed in an end to the world. But it doesn't mean that the enemy wishes to keep blowing smoke up our nostrils," Tony explained.

"That's skirt, you Brit," Derek joked.

"Whose skirt are you talking about?" Tony clearly didn't understand the reference, but they went back to the broadcast.

"Well, there you have it, folks. Our experts are nearly sure that your pain will reduce significantly in about six months from the date that you were stung by the Whites, which could be as little as a few weeks from now.

"The Greys are voraciously trying to protect us in the spirit realm, but these so-Called Saints need to be eradicated. I have just been given instructions in my headset," James touched his ear to listen. "Anyone who is found without the Marker on his arm or forehead may be shot on sight. It used to be the purview of the Hunters who were seeking that reward, but we need all hands on deck to curb the blight upon humanity. These believers of a false Christ need to be gunned down on the streets. There will be no questions asked, as long as they have no Marker on them. Go ahead and shoot to your heart's content. You have seen the evidence, and they deserve it. Their betrayal will meet with a bitter end."

CHAPTER NINETEEN

As they neared the end of the fourth month, scenes of shootings on the streets were more common. Those infected souls, destined for Hell based upon their Marker, were amazed that the Called Saints could be killed. There was no pulse or breath from the people they could kill, but still none of the stung could complete the transition into eternity, so that their agony could end. But, it didn't mean that Hunters wouldn't try.

All over the streets of the world, blathering decapitated heads were still moving, while their bodies lie lifeless nearby. Even if the head was smashed, the eyes were still processing sensations and peering out in their horror regarding their final existence. The Hunters worked tirelessly, through their pain, to kill off the Called Saints of God.

Some in the media began to speculate that the Called Saints were given an antidote to create zombies out of the law-abiding citizens of the globe. They were then openly tortured, without mercy, until the Hunters finally killed the poor soul in front of the crowds that cursed them in their death throes.

But another problem started to pop up only a month later. Those who were at their worst of the undead existence progressed toward lifelessness. The new reality of those dying was met with levels of trepidation and suspicion by the unliving dying or the tormented wounded. Physicians and nurses began to examine the corpses and noted that death had accomplished its cycle. Praise to their god, Cartiff, was on their lips each time another one died in supposed peace.

Derek was physically wavering. He wondered if he was in the next batch to die but refused to entertain the thought for anything more than a few moments. Tarra continued to tirelessly keep the Ranch going on a subsistence level, while Derek could just read on the couch and move his legs to keep from bedsores or blood pooling along his bottom. He could achieve no more than a few leg lifts and shift in his weakened state. In an ordinary world, he would have been in the hospital with significant medical care. In the last week of the possible onset of the Zombie Trumpet, as the Called Saints referred to the murderous time without the death, very few had much energy of any type.

When Tarra fed Derek his second meal of the day, trying to get him to eat small portions over six times a day, she moved to Charlene to note that she was lolled over to the side more than usual. When she could induce no physiological response, she began to hang her hands to her side in despair, believing that she had succumbed to her many suicide attempts. Only when Dr. Tony arrived an hour later did he confirm that Charlene had died. The whole group was terribly conflicted by Charlene's passing. In their hearts, they all knew she had consigned herself to the portion of eternity without redemption.

Derek asked many questions of Tony, who only had a few answers about Hell, other than its finality of the decision. He found several eBooks on the Two Witness' site that answered many of his queries, confirming where he then knew his mother had gone. That fact drove him to pray for an opportunity to be bold for his faith. He wondered how he would do it from the couch with only Tarra around. The TV again clicked on reminding them that they hadn't disconnected their sixty-five inch screen from the automated news channel, WNN.

"We interrupt our broadcast shows about the splendid opinions of our messiah's work in rebuilding the world to give you this special announcement: many are dead on the streets of our nations. They woke up this Monday morning with a little more energy than they had in all of the past months, but as they reached the public and private transportations, at approximately nine AM Eastern time, they collapsed. Medical examiners on the scenes indicate the most massive death toll in human history, happened in a single hour. It would be excellent work of our government and the Greys, if it weren't so tragic to lose our brothers and sisters around the globe.

"We estimate that more than one hundred million may have died, but that approximation has to be on the extreme low end. We won't know more until full tallies are tabulated. Do not ask for a coroner. We are giving people instructions to bury them at least six feet under to reduce the spread of disease, or to put the deceased in large garbage bags taped up to seal in the incredible smell that will surely arise in our cities. As you know, garbage workers are in short supply. We will keep you informed..." Derek muted the TV, as he felt his heart race with Tarra laying in his arms.

She could not stand the smell of his decaying body, so she chose not to bath herself and sprayed cologne on both of them. With those two conditions, their nostrils were given a break, because both reeked to high heaven. She felt the heartbeat of Derek become erratic and raised herself off of his chest.

"Derek! What is it?" Tarra jumped to her feet in alarm.

"Oh man, I thought so," Derek weakly answered.

"What!?" Tarra begged.

"I died many months ago, and now I must die," Derek's eyes rolled back into their sockets, as he gave up the oddest fight in one's life. Tarra knew that this might be the realm of all who had bled out or had tried to kill themselves during this time of evil which she learned was only the Fifth Trumpet. The Sixth Trumpet was sure to blow soon enough.

Tony and Heather came to bury the mother and son beside each other in the backyard. The couple held Tarra in a three-way embrace of brothers and sisters, realizing that Derek was in the arms of Jesus. Only days later, news sources would reveal that the death toll had reached more than three hundred million worldwide.

"No other war in human history took a greater toll on the lives of the people than the Great Zombie Trumpet." Tony exclaimed from the backseat of their SUV traveling for the last of the trips from the Ranch, which had been Tarra's home for almost a year.

"How can the world survive anything more horrific than this torturous death at the hands of themselves? It was a massive planet wide suicide," Tarra intoned giving place to the thought that they all considered.

"What's the Sixth Trumpet again, honey?" Heather looked into the rear view mirror to her beloved husband, whom she only married after the Rapture of the Church occurred almost six years earlier.

"From my calculations of Revelation 9:15-16, and some insights from the PlanBible.com's ministry I was reading, it states the following: 'So the four angels who were prepared for the hour, day, month, and year were released to kill a third of the human race. The number of the mounted troops was 200 million; I heard their number.'"

"What does that mean?" Tarra leaned backward to ask.

"It means that *The War to End All Wars* will begin within days. It's the only place in the Bible that mentions an exact moment in time. I have prayed about this and looked it up on several sites to verify it. I believe that it shows that God has always had a plan for the exact date of the Sixth Trumpet since before the foundation of the earth. It was planned, and no one could forestall it. But I kinda wish that I didn't have to be here for it," Tony answered lost in his thoughts.

"So, what you are saying is that God planned the Sixth Trumpet from before the beginning of the universe for a time just a few days or weeks from now? How can He figure that part out? There has to be literally billions of combinations to consider. That boggles my mind." Heather answered her almost unanswerable question as she pulled into their house, bringing Tarra home as their spiritual niece.

"What's amazing to answer is that Jesus did all of this for us. He was considering me at the time that the universe began when he ordered the days," Tony stated the sober comment echoed in their brains, as they moved Tarra into her new bedroom.

Over the next week, the three began to pull the tomatoes and potatoes from their large garden, with a keen eye upon the news, waiting for the moment that the Sixth Trumpet began. Since the other Trumpet blasts were spiritual in nature when the angels blew their instruments, they did not expect that the four angels held back for the exact moment in time would be visible. But the moment would be indelibly written upon humanity when the nuclear plumes were first seen over Moscow sparking the latest War to End All Wars. Only the Called Saints knew better.

ABOUT THE AUTHOR

Dr. Scott Young, CCC-A, FAAA, an Audiologist since 1991, and owns Hearing Solution Centers, Inc. in Tulsa, OK. Besides World War II studies, his passions include writing, Sci-Fi and singing. He has written a fictional novel, *The Violin's Secret*, which chronicles the survival of one young teenager through the Holocaust. *Singing in the Mind: A Study of the Voice and Song* was his first non-fictional writing about the passion of singing and a different view of how singing occurs in the mind and its role in the culture.

Professor in History was his third, but second fictional book of a man who is an atheist but has the fantastic opportunity to ask Jesus unique questions on various topics. *ForeTold - Book 1 and 2* will be out soon. It chronicles the End of the Earth from a Biblical perspective in a fictional form.

More information can be found at www.DrScottYoung.com. Dr. Young is a unique communicator in the way he perceives the world, as his wife, Wendy, and his son, Stefan, will attest. My thanks go to Wendy and Kim McCarty, who read this book quite thoroughly to find my errors.

Made in the USA
Las Vegas, NV
17 April 2022